Katie let out a screech as the cold, sticky liquid oozed its way down her face and all over her expensive yellow suit.

"Why don't you look where you're—" She looked up into the eyes of the stranger and realized. . .he wasn't a stranger at all.

Karl.

She watched his expression change—from one of embarrassment to shock. Or was it horror? She couldn't be quite sure. Either way, he looked like he wanted to bolt. Just like she'd done all those years ago.

If Katie could have avoided this day for the rest of her life, she would have. She had managed for twelve years, hadn't she?

JANICE A. THOMPSON is a Christian author from Texas. She has four grown daughters, and the whole family is active in ministry, particularly the arts. Janice is a writer by trade but wears many other hats, as well. She previously taught drama and creative writing at a Christian school of the arts. She also directed a global drama missions team. She currently spends her days bouncing back and forth between editing, writing, and public speaking. Janice is passionate about her faith and does all she can to share it with others, which is why she particularly loves writing inspirational novels. Through her stories, she hopes to lead others into a relationship with a loving God.

Books by Janice A. Thompson

HEARTSONG PRESENTS
HP490—A Class of Her Own
HP593—Angel Incognito
HP613—A Chorus of One
HP666—Sweet Charity
HP667—Banking on Love
HP734—Larkspur Dreams (coauthored with Anita Higman)
HP754—Red Like Crimson
HP778—The Love Song (coauthored with Anita Higman)
HP786—White as Snow

Don't miss out on any of our super romances. Write to us at the following address for information on our newest releases and club information.

Heartsong Presents Readers' Service
PO Box 721
Uhrichsville, OH 44683

Or visit www.heartsongpresents.com

Out of
the Blue

Janice A. Thompson

Heartsong Presents

To my sister, Connie: How wonderful it must be—living so close to those breathtaking Amish farms! Thanks for that fun trip to Lancaster County last spring. I had a great time, and it was even more special because I got to share it with you and Mom.

A note from the Author:
I love to hear from my readers! You may correspond with me by writing:

Janice A. Thompson
Author Relations
PO Box 721
Uhrichsville, OH 44683

ISBN 978-1-60260-057-7

OUT OF THE BLUE

Our mission is to publish and distribute inspirational products offering exceptional value and biblical encouragement to the masses.

PRINTED IN THE U.S.A.

prologue

Paradise, Pennsylvania

"Stand still, Katie, or I might accidentally stick you with a pin."

Katie Walken stopped her twisting and turning long enough for her mother to finish pinning up the carefully measured hem of her new dress. She let out an exaggerated sigh, wishing she could be anywhere but here. Why Mamm and Aunt Emma had chosen Friday, her busiest day at the store, to finish a simple sewing project was beyond her.

She glanced down at the navy blue broadcloth and sighed. It hung heavy on her, like a weight, a burden in need of lifting. Oh, how she wished she could wear a pair of jeans and a T-shirt, like so many of the English girls who came into the store. And if only she could cut her cumbersome mane of brown hair into one of those trendy styles, tossing her white kapp for good. . . then she would be happy.

The last few weeks had been filled with such longings. Katie pushed them aside at first, remembering her obligations, her strict Amish upbringing. But now, as the summertime crowd of tourists made their way through Lancaster County, as the outside world merged with her own once again, she could avoid the inevitable no longer. Katie ached for what she could not have—the life of an Englisher. One free of pointless restrictions.

Like this ridiculous blue dress.

The rocker in the corner creaked as her aunt Emma eased her weight back and forth, back and forth. "I wore that same shade of blue on my wedding day," she said with a smile. "I was just eighteen, like you."

"I'm not quite eighteen yet," Katie replied as she gave one of the sleeves a tug. "And I'm not altogether sure I will ever marry, in this dress or any other." She continued to pull at the fabric, wondering why it seemed to stifle her breathing.

"Of course you will!" Her mother eased another pin into the sturdy cloth. "Karl Borg will ask you to be his as soon as you turn eighteen." She gave Katie a little wink. "That boy has been smitten with you for as long as I can remember."

"Everyone in Paradise knows the two of you will marry in the fall," Aunt Emma concurred.

Katie did her best not to groan. Karl was her best friend, to be sure. Their mutual affection had started in childhood and lingered still. She'd watched his sparkling blue eyes twinkle with mischief many times over the years as they'd played together. But marriage?

Mamm reached for another pin. "Your father says Karl has already come to him, asking for permission. Why do you think we must hurry with the dress?"

Hearing this news almost knocked the breath out of Katie. Right away, her hands began to tremble. "What did Datt say?"

"He will give his permission as soon as you are baptized and join the church." Her mother's eyes watered. "And I will wait for that day with a joyful heart. To think, my daughter will be happily married before the year's end."

She dove into a lengthy conversation about the many benefits of a godly marriage, but Katie found herself lost in the words. All she could think about—all she would ever again be able to think about—was Karl Borg's visit to her father. . .and what she could do to stop this wedding from ever taking place.

one

Doylestown, Pennsylvania, twelve years later

Katie leaned back in her chair and glanced at the calendar on the wall. Friday. Funny how she could never keep one day straight from another. With such a hectic schedule, remembering the names of her clients—and the addresses of her listings—took all of her energy. She couldn't be expected to remember the day of the week on top of everything else, could she?

Not that she minded the busyness, really. Filling the days with work certainly beat the alternative: quiet solitude. Too much time to think, especially about the past, wasn't a good thing.

For a moment, she allowed her mind to slip back to the farm, to a quieter, simpler life. It seemed like a hundred years had passed between then and now. Had she really left all of that peacefulness behind, swapping it out for a chaotic lifestyle, one she could barely keep up with?

For a moment, she allowed her thoughts to go there. To Paradise. Just as quickly, she shifted back to reality. In an attempt to distract herself, Katie gazed around her office, taking in the beautiful decor. She couldn't help but wonder what her parents would think if they saw all of this, especially the framed artwork on the walls. Such luxuries were forbidden among the Amish.

But the furniture would hold some appeal, especially

to her father. The mahogany bookshelves. The matching credenza. The fabulous desk with its glass top. Such beautiful craftsmanship. Then again, Katie wouldn't have it any other way. These furnishings—which she had chosen with great care—made her feel at home.

The blinking of the cursor on the computer screen beckoned, and Katie shifted gears. She spent a few minutes entering some necessary information and uploading a few photos of an exquisite lakefront property she'd just listed, one complete with a spacious five-bedroom house. She also chose a new photo of herself, one recently taken, to replace her old one on the company's site.

She stared at it for a moment. The woman in the picture smiled back at her with a white-toothed smile, her green eyes sparkling, her yellow linen suit freshly pressed, and her shoulder-length hair styled in the latest fashion. Yes, she looked quite professional. And why not? You had to put your best foot forward in real estate if you wanted to garner the top clientele.

After finishing up on the Internet, Katie checked her voice mail. Only six messages this time. Three pressing. Two not so pressing. One from a former client, asking for a date. Nothing new there. He'd been at it for several weeks. How long she could continue putting him off was yet to be seen.

"Hey, girl!"

A voice at the door distracted Katie from the phone. She glanced up to discover her coworker Aimee Riley. The petite blond looked especially pretty today in dark slacks and a sky blue blouse. Katie couldn't help but wonder what Aunt Emma would think of that particular shade of blue.

"Hey, I'm surprised to see you here." Katie turned her attentions back to her friend. "Did you skip lunch?"

"Yeah, I was busy," Aimee said with a shrug. "Had about a dozen calls to make. I'm following a couple of pretty good leads."

"I've been busy, too." Katie grinned. "Just uploaded some new photos to our Web site. You'll have to sign online in a few minutes and check them out."

"I heard." Her coworker gave an approving nod. "Congratulations on your new listing. I hear that's a million-dollar property you just signed."

"A million *two*." Katie corrected her with a playful wink.

Aimee dropped into the wingback chair in the corner and sighed. "Must be nice."

"Yes." Katie closed the laptop and gazed into her friend's eyes. "It's a great place, Aimee, and I'm so blessed to get it. There's the most amazing house on multiple acres of land. On the lake. And here's the thing—with the market so hot right now, I'm convinced it'll pull in more than the asking price. I'm hoping for at least another hundred thousand before all is said and done."

"Man." Aimee shook her head. "I wouldn't mind taking home 6 percent of a million three."

Katie chuckled. "Well, get busy! Find me a buyer, and we'll split the commission." She reached into the desk drawer and came up with a tube of lip gloss, which she liberally applied to her parched lips.

"You've got a deal. I'll give it my best shot, anyway." Aimee paused and glanced down the hallway before asking, "Does Hannah know?"

"Are you kidding?" Katie put the lip gloss away. "Of course. She's always the first to know everything around here."

"That cousin of yours is a real pistol," Aimee said. "Ever since she made office manager, she. . ."

"I what, Aimee?" Hannah appeared in the doorway with an inquisitive look on her face. The slightly overweight thirty-something folded her arms at her chest, lips pursed.

"Um, you've turned this whole company around," Aimee said with a nod.

"That's more like it." Hannah's frown eased its way into a smile.

Katie couldn't help but smile, too. In spite of her cousin's tough exterior, Hannah really had done a great job of getting Bucks County Realty back on its feet. Excellent at keeping things—and people—in order, Hannah made a top-notch manager. If only the same positive comments could be made concerning her rowdy children and messy home.

Aunt Emma would surely cluck her tongue in disapproval at her oldest daughter's habits. Then again, the conservative older woman would likely disapprove of a great many things that went on in Hannah's house—like fast food for dinner, piles of laundry on the floor, excessive television watching, and children who talked back to their parents when they didn't get what they wanted.

"I just came in to tell you that a new client is on his way." Hannah's words drew Katie back to the present. "An investor, looking to buy up several farms in the area."

"An investor?" Katie drew in a deep breath. "What is he going to do with all of those properties?" She dreaded hearing the answer. For months now, investors had been sweeping in, buying up prime farmland to build apartments, housing developments, and so forth. Parking lots now reigned supreme, taking the place of the quaint farms of the past.

For that matter, many things from Katie's past had been replaced, hadn't they?

She shrugged off her sadness and turned back to her

cousin with a strained smile.

"I don't have a clue." Hannah shrugged. "I just know he's interested in the Chandler place, and that's worth a pretty penny. He also mentioned something about that piece of property off on Wilcox, as well as a couple of others."

Katie's eyes widened. "Are you serious?"

"I'm serious." Hannah looked back and forth between the two Realtors. "So, which of you ladies wants to court this gentleman?"

There was something about the word "court" that didn't sit well with Katie. She made a quick decision to step aside and let her coworker take this one. "I just got that new listing," she explained with an easy lilt to her voice. "Why don't you take this guy, Aimee? The Chandler place is yours, anyway."

Her friend's eyes lit up and excitement laced her words. "Are you sure?"

"Yes. I'm going to have my hands full trying to sweep buyers off their feet with this new lakefront property."

"If you say so." Aimee turned back toward the door, almost tripping over her own feet. She looked over at Hannah and asked, "When is he coming in?"

"I told him to be here at four."

"That's less than an hour." With a flustered look on her face, Aimee headed out into the hallway then circled around to pose one more question. "Oh. I forgot to ask. . . .What's the guy's name?"

Hannah glanced down at the papers in her hand. "I'm pretty sure he said his last name is Borg," she said. "I wrote it down. Hang on." She looked a little closer at the paper, and her eyes grew wide.

"What is it, Hannah?" Aimee asked.

Hannah looked over at Katie, her face turning pale. "I just

realized why this name sounded so familiar." After a brief pause, she stammered, "It–it's Karl. Karl Borg."

Karl Borg? Katie's stomach twisted in knots the moment she heard the familiar name. Could it possibly be the same man?

Regardless, she found herself wanting to run—to leave the building before he arrived. She'd managed it twelve years ago, hadn't she? Slipping out of her bedroom window in the cool of night had been her mode of operation then.

Avoiding him today might prove to be a little trickier. The windows at Bucks County Realty were far too small—and she might mess up her designer suit.

❧

Karl exited his sports car just outside the office of Bucks County Realty with his briefcase in hand. Slipping away from his law office midafternoon had been a challenge, but he'd finally managed to get here, albeit five minutes late. He paused as he caught a glimpse of his reflection in the glass front door. The wind had done quite a number on his hair. Setting his briefcase on the ground, Karl ran his fingers through the choppy strands then straightened his tie.

Seconds later, he entered the foyer of the Realtor's office. Once inside, he approached the receptionist at the front desk and asked to speak to Aimee Riley, the woman he'd been referred to. He hoped he had landed with just the right agent. Several pieces of property interested him at the moment, and he prayed he would get the best possible deal on each of them. He would need a savvy Realtor to accomplish that.

As he waited, the receptionist offered him a cup of coffee, which he willingly accepted. He added a couple of packets of sugar then gave it a stir. After a busy day and no lunch break, he certainly needed the caffeine.

One sip, however, convinced him otherwise. The murky

liquid tasted burnt. Ironic, since it wasn't even warm. Unsure of what to do with it, he set it on a small end table and continued to wait. Moments later, a pretty blond appeared in the lobby with a broad smile on her face. "Mr. Borg, I'm Aimee Riley." She extended her hand, and he shook it. "Please, follow me to my office."

He grabbed his briefcase then pondered his dilemma as he looked at the cup of coffee. If he refused it, the receptionist's feelings might be hurt. If he took it, he might actually have to drink it. With his free hand, he reached to snatch it up then trailed the Realtor down a long, narrow hallway.

They entered her office, and Karl looked around in awe. He placed the cup of coffee on the edge of the glass-topped desk and gestured to the artwork on the walls. "This is really nice," he said. "Reminds me of home."

"Oh? Do you collect Keller's paintings, too?" she asked.

"No." He couldn't help but smile. "I grew up in a house that looked like that." He pointed to the farmhouse in one of the paintings.

"Oh, I see." She gave him a nod. "Well, I'm glad you like it. We'll take that as a confirmation that you've chosen the right Realtor." She sat at her desk and gestured for him to take the seat across from her. "I just hung the pictures a couple of weeks ago. It was pretty plain in here before that."

Plain.

As he sat, Karl drew in a deep breath, forcing images from his past behind. All memories of life on the farm brought back painful recollections of the day his world had changed forever. The day the woman he thought he would marry had sprinted out of his life, leaving him in the dust. He shook off the memory and placed his briefcase in the empty chair to his right.

With determination eking from every pore, he focused on the task set before him. "I'm here to talk with you about several pieces of property I'm interested in purchasing. I am particularly interested in the listing on Chandler," he explained. "It's a beautiful piece of farmland, but it's been on the market more than ninety days."

"Right."

"I plan to make an offer, but it will be far below the asking price."

He reached for the coffee cup, forgetting it was undrinkable until he'd swallowed a mouthful of the nasty stuff. He tried not to let it show on his face as he put the cup back down once again.

"Ah." She nodded. "I took a couple of clients out there just last week. I think the asking price is a bit high, and I'm sure the owners—an older couple—will come down if pressed. They're running behind on their mortgage, so if we move quickly, we might be able to make them an offer they can't refuse."

His heart lurched as the news of the late mortgage registered. "If no one buys, will they lose the place to foreclosure?"

"Likely." She shrugged. "But who knows. These farmers are up one minute, down the next, depending on the weather."

"And a host of other things," he interjected.

His mind took him back to that awful day, just weeks after his parents' deaths. As an only child, selling the farm had been his only real option. Karl had sprinted from Paradise— almost as fast as Katie.

"I listed the property several months ago, and there haven't been many showings." Aimee continued on, clearly oblivious to his thoughts. "So the goal here is to get it sold at a price everyone can live with."

They wrapped up their meeting in short order, and Karl stood to shake Aimee's hand. "You've been very helpful." He offered her a warm smile.

"I hope things end as well as they've started," she responded. "You never know what's going to happen in real estate. A situation can look like it's all wrapped up one minute, then be up in the air the next."

Her statement left him feeling a little discombobulated. Isn't that just what had happened in his life? His whole life in Paradise felt completely "wrapped up" as she had said. And then, in one swift move, it had all come crashing down.

With a sigh, Karl leaned down to pick up his briefcase with one hand. Noticing the still-full cup of cold coffee, he reached to grab it, as well. He could always toss it when he got outside.

Aimee ushered him out into the hallway, and just as they neared the lobby, another woman entered the narrow space, papers in hand. He couldn't really get a good look at the brunette's face. She appeared to be focused on the documents she carried, not paying a bit of attention to her surroundings. Karl tried to shift to the right at the last moment, realizing she was going to hit him head-on if he didn't dodge her.

Unfortunately, he didn't quite make it.

The clipboard in her hand turned out to be just the right height to take out his cup of coffee. The Styrofoam cup shot from his hand, straight up into the air, then back down again.

Landing right on top of her head.

two

Katie let out a screech as the cold, sticky liquid oozed its way down her face and all over her expensive yellow suit. "Why don't you look where you're—" She looked up into the eyes of the stranger and realized. . .he wasn't a stranger at all.

Karl.

She watched his expression change—from one of embarrassment to shock. Or was it horror? She couldn't be quite sure. Either way, he looked like he wanted to bolt. Just like she'd done all those years ago.

If Katie could have avoided this day for the rest of her life, she would have. She had managed for twelve years, hadn't she?

Hoping to distract herself, she dropped to her knees to rescue the papers, which now lined the hallway. The coffee had done a number on those, too. They trembled in her hand as she fetched them.

Within seconds, Karl bent to his knees to offer assistance. "Katie, I. . .I'm so sorry."

"No, it's my fault." She looked into his beautiful blue eyes and instantly felt herself transported back in time twelve years. No, further than that. These were the same mischievous eyes that had drawn her in as a young girl, had wooed her to befriend a pesky neighbor boy who loved nothing more than to tease and torment her with frogs and lizards.

Hmm. He didn't appear to be hiding any of those in his pockets today, did he?

No, she had to admit. Looking at him now, tall and solidly built with his tailored suit and stylish haircut, he looked to be quite the professional. Clearly, he had left the old ways behind, as well. But when? And why? Had her impulsive actions resulted in that, too?

With his help, she managed to gather up the soggy papers and then stand. His hand—the same hand that had reached to take hers as they crossed the narrow bridge over Pequea Creek all those years ago—steadied her now as she rose to her feet.

"Thank you," she managed. The heat in her cheeks alarmed her, but not as much as the thought of what she must look like right now. She reached up to touch her hair then groaned. "I. . .I have to go take care of this. I look. . ."

"Amazing," he whispered. Then his cheeks reddened. He raked his fingers through his blond hair, and his gaze shifted to the ground.

Katie turned toward the ladies' room.

Aimee followed on her heels. "Katie? Want me to come with you?"

"No, I'm fine."

As she rounded the corner, she had to admit. . .she wasn't fine. In fact, after looking into Karl Borg's striking blue eyes, Katie wondered if she would ever be fine again.

❧

Karl paced the foyer of Bucks County Realty, his mind reeling. For years he had attempted to push all thoughts of Katie Walken out of his mind. He'd done a pretty good job, too. Karl had nearly forgotten how pretty she looked when she got riled up. How the sunlight played with the fine strands of blond in her brunette hair. How the early summer sun gave rise to a smattering of freckles on the end of her nose.

But now, seeing those green eyes, hearing the sound of her voice, feeling the touch of her hand in his. . . Surely he would have to work overtime to rid himself of these new feelings that flooded over him.

In all the scenarios he had imagined in his mind, he'd never come close to this. His Katie—once tall and slim with brunette hair pulled back under her kapp—now wore perfectly applied eyeliner and mascara. Her cheeks, once sun-kissed, now shimmered with a store-bought blush, and her full lips, the same lips he had dreamed of kissing for years, were covered in a soft pink gloss.

And that outfit! How she carried herself in it, like a woman, not a girl. Karl didn't remember her curves being quite so pronounced, but then again, under the straight dresses she'd always worn back in Lancaster County, he wouldn't have.

He closed his eyes and tried to remember what she used to look like then opened them again to merge the two images in his brain. Nope. It wouldn't compute.

And yet he'd seen it with his own eyes. Katie Walken—all grown up and looking like something straight off the pages of a fashion magazine.

Aimee interrupted his thoughts. "Mr. Borg, would you like another cup of coffee?"

"No thanks." He continued to pace, trying to make sense out of this. Katie worked in a realty office. She sold property. He bought property. It was inevitable they would eventually meet, right? Surely this was all just some crazy coincidence.

On the other hand, he didn't really believe in coincidences, did he? Most of the coincidental things in his life had proven to be God-incidences, after all. Karl pondered that possibility. Had the Lord moved him to Doylestown to find Katie again? And if so, did she even *want* to be found?

He took a seat in one of the large wingback chairs and tapped his fingers on the end table, trying to figure out what, if anything, to do.

"I'm sure Katie will be fine," Aimee said with a reassuring smile. "There's really no reason for you to stay."

"I have to."

"Oh. . .okay." She gave him a curious look then shrugged. "I have some work to do. If you don't mind. . ."

"No, go ahead. But, please, would you let Katie know that I'm not leaving until I talk to her? I'll sit here all day if I have to."

"Um, sure." Aimee shrugged. "Whatever you say."

As she rounded the corner, Karl called out, "Aimee?"

She returned right away. "Yes?"

"There wouldn't happen to be a window in that bathroom, would there?" He began to rap his fingers on the end table once again as his nerves kicked in.

"Well, yes, I think so," she said, looking confused. "Why?"

"Oh, no reason." He leaned back against the chair and drew in a deep sigh. "No reason at all."

❧

Katie stood in front of the bathroom mirror and worked feverishly to get the stains out of her jacket. Not that it mattered. Even if she got it back in shape, she could do little about her hair.

Gazing at her reflection, she groaned. She wouldn't want to be seen by anyone in this condition, especially not Karl.

Tears sprang to her eyes, and she dabbed them away with a piece of toilet paper. No point in getting emotional. It certainly wouldn't make things any better, would it? And besides, the past was in the past.

Giving up on the jacket, she took a paper towel and tried

to dab at her hair. Hanging her head upside down might be her best choice. She flung her hair forward and tipped over, then took the paper towel and began to work it through the matted strands in an attempt to soak up some of the moisture.

Just then, she heard a rap on the door.

"Katie?" Aimee stepped inside the room and closed the door behind her.

"Aimee, I'll explain later." Katie continued on in her upsidedown position, hoping her friend would give her some time alone to get her thoughts straight—to figure out why the Lord had suddenly dropped Karl back into her life once again, after all these years.

"I just wanted to tell you that Mr. Borg is waiting up front for you."

Katie groaned and stood aright. "Maybe he'll go away if I stay in here long enough." She began to work her hair into place with her fingers, but it didn't want to cooperate.

"He's not going anywhere," Aimee explained, her brow still wrinkled in concern. "He said he would sit out there all day if he had to."

Another groan escaped Katie's lips. So, Karl hadn't changed. He'd always had the patience of a saint. Just one more area where they were polar opposites.

Her thoughts slipped back in time to another day when he had waited on her for hours. They were supposed to meet at the edge of the creek to go fishing at seven in the morning. Katie's mother had given her more chores than usual that morning, and she didn't make it until ten thirty. But there he sat, hat on his head, pole in his hand, legs slung over the edge of the creek, as if he had nothing better to do than spend three and a half hours waiting on her.

On the other hand, he'd managed to catch quite a few fish in her absence that day.

Still, with the sharp business suit he now wore, he likely had far more to do than sit in the front lobby of Bucks County Realty waiting on an old flame.

Hmm. Maybe flame wasn't the right word. They'd never even kissed, after all.

She tried to avoid her friend's expression, but Aimee made it difficult. Her penetrating gaze was tough to ignore.

"So, are you going to tell me what's going on, or am I going to have to guess?"

"He. . .he's just someone I used to know." Katie took another glance in the mirror. "From my former life."

"Ah. Well, he's certainly got you all shook up. There's got to be a reason why."

"I'm just embarrassed, is all. It's not every day I bathe in coffee."

"I'll admit the whole thing was plenty embarrassing." Aimee folded her arms at her chest and shook her head. "But there's more to it than that. Did you used to date this guy?"

"I can say in all honesty that I *never* dated Karl Borg." No lying there. Teens in her conservative Amish community hadn't dated, at least not in the traditional sense. Unless you called a buggy ride a date. Or a quiet walk after a barn raising.

"Hmm." Aimee reached over and straightened the back of Katie's collar, then stepped back to give her a once-over. "You never dated him, and yet your eyes lit up the moment you recognized him. Very suspicious."

My eyes lit up? Katie pondered that for a second. There had been a moment of recognition but nothing more. Except, perhaps, fear.

After drawing in a deep breath, she turned to face her friend, ready to deal with the obvious. "I'm going out there."

"I wish I could come, too. I would pay money to hear this conversation."

"I'll fill you in later. I promise." Katie reached to open the bathroom door then took a tentative step into the hall. Then another. And another. All the way to the lobby, she debated what she would say once she saw him.

Maybe it would be better not to plan anything out—just let nature take its course when the moment came.

On the other hand. . .as she rounded the corner into the lobby and took one look at Karl with that boyish face of his, only one thing came to mind. She wanted to give him her hand and let him guide her across the bridge at Pequea Creek one more time, for old time's sake. Surely once would be enough to stop this crazy pounding in her heart.

three

Karl stood the moment Katie entered the room. He tried to squelch the anxiety that rushed over him as he stared into her beautiful face. She had changed in so many ways, and yet underneath that polished, coffee-coated exterior, the old Katie remained. Driven. Excited about life. Ready to take on the world.

As she drew near, Karl tried to figure out what to do. Should he embrace her? After all, they were old friends. Old friends met with a hug, didn't they? At least among the Englishers. She reached out first, slipping an arm around his waist. He drew her close, and they remained, if only for a second.

Katie stepped back all too quickly, and he noticed the fear in her eyes. Would she find an excuse to shoot out of the front door or give him a few moments to ask the questions that had been nagging at him for years?

"I. . .um. . .was just about to leave for the day." She glanced up at the clock on the wall, and he followed her gaze. 5:24.

"I can't just leave without talking to you." He gave her his best pleading look. "Couldn't we please go out for—" He started to say "a cup of coffee" but stopped himself after thinking better of it. She'd already had enough coffee for one day. "Maybe a bite to eat?"

"I don't know." Katie paused and ran her fingers through her hair. "I look like a wreck."

"You look wonderful," he managed.

Her cheeks flushed pink, just as they had done a hundred times as a little girl when he'd teased her. Only now, she didn't seem to mind his comments. In fact, she seemed to soften more as time went on.

"Just a few minutes to talk?" He tried again.

As she nodded, a wave of relief washed over him. Maybe he would get the answers he had been seeking, after all.

"Let me just run back to my office and grab my purse," she said. "I'll have to shut down my computer and turn out the lights, so it might take a couple of minutes."

"I'll wait."

"Or you could come with." She gestured toward the hall, and he followed along behind her like a puppy dog.

His eyes grew large as they entered her spacious office. "This is amazing, Katie." He approached the mahogany bookshelf unit. "The craftsmanship on this piece is beautiful."

She smiled and her cheeks turned pink. "I've always wondered what you might think of it. Your woodworking skills were the best in Lancaster County."

"Hardly." He laughed. "But I could definitely see myself working on something like this." He drew in a deep breath and added, "In another life, I mean."

"I hear ya." She reached over to turn off her computer, and the room fell silent. Karl tried to cover up the awkwardness by looking at the pictures on the bookshelf. His heart nearly shifted to his toes as he came across a photo of three small children. Strange. He'd never thought to look at Katie's left hand for a ring. If she had children, surely she had to be married.

Thankfully, she took note of his interest in the photograph and offered up a more palatable explanation. "What do you think of my cousin's children? Aren't they cute?"

Karl tried not to the let the relief show in his eyes as he turned back toward her. "They're a nice-looking crew. The little girl reminds me of you at that age." He looked again at the photograph, realizing the child wore modern English clothes and had a stylish haircut. "Except for a few obvious things." He turned to give Katie a warm smile. "She does have the same batch of freckles on the end of her nose, just like you."

Katie groaned as she reached for her purse. "I always hated those freckles."

"I didn't. I used to count them."

Her gaze shifted down to some papers on the desk, which she rearranged. "The little girl's name is Madison. She's the spitting image of her mother." Katie looked up, locking eyes with him. "You remember my cousin, Hannah, right? Aunt Emma's daughter?"

"The one who ran away when she was eighteen and married the English boy?" he asked. Karl wished he could take the words back as quickly as they were spoken, but there was no swallowing them now that they were out.

"Yes. She met him during her *rumspringa*, while visiting friends in Doylestown," Katie explained. "And tried to fight her feelings for him. I think she must have convinced herself she could overcome her love for him, because she was baptized as soon as she returned home, made her commitment to the church."

Karl knew what that meant of course. Once an Amish teen made the decision to be baptized, it was a public covenant to the Amish way of life. . .forever. To leave after making such a declaration would result in only one thing, at least in their Order.

"Less than a month after her joining the church, Matt

showed up, completely brokenhearted. Told her that he couldn't live without her." Katie sighed. "I remember how torn she was over the decision. Despite her attempts to the contrary, her love for him proved to be very strong. And yet she knew if she left after joining the church, she would be—"

"Shunned."

"Yes, and it's so sad," Katie explained, "because Matt's a great guy, and he really loves the Lord. I think the decision to leave Paradise nearly killed Hannah, but she did it out of love for him."

"I understand that kind of love." His gaze shifted downward as soon as the words slipped out. Though he had not planned to convey such feelings, they obviously could not be held back. After a few seconds, he garnered the courage to look back up into Katie's eyes.

"Love is a powerful thing," she continued.

"And it often calls for sacrifice," he added. *At least from my experience.*

"Yes, well. . .Hannah did sacrifice a lot. She had to give up one family to gain another."

"Sad."

"Well, most of the story is happy. She and Matt got married and settled in Doylestown, near his family. They're both great people, very active in their local church. I've just always hated it that they can't go back home to see her family. I know she's thinking about it. From what I hear, many of the Amish are softening their stance on shunning. I've heard of a great many Amish teens leaving after their baptism then being welcomed back at weddings and funerals and so forth."

"I've heard the same." He had always balked at the idea of shunning those who left the community but had kept his opinions to himself. Secretly, he had been relieved that Katie had sneaked away before her baptism, realizing it left the door open for her return. She could go back if she wanted to.

Not that it looked like she wanted to.

He thought back to the events surrounding her leaving. Getting the news early in the morning. Hoping, praying, it was some sort of joke on her part. Waiting for days to hear something, anything. Finally getting the message about her trek to Doylestown to stay with extended family members.

Oh, how he had prayed during those days and weeks following her abrupt exit from Paradise. How he had fought the urge to run after her, to plead with her to come back—not just to him, but to the quiet, simple life they would live together.

As he gazed into her eyes now, Karl had to admit she seemed better suited to this fast-paced lifestyle. Perhaps she had found her niche, after all.

Maybe she'd found someone to love, as well.

He gave the bookshelf unit a quick glance, in search of another photo. Thankfully, he found nothing but real estate books and knickknacks. He looked at her left hand, praying he would not find a ring.

No ring.

Just then, Katie crossed the room in his direction to turn off the light. For a moment, she and Karl stood quite close in the semidarkened room, almost close enough to reach out and touch one another. He struggled with the feelings that gripped him at her nearness.

With resolve building, he took a step backward, giving her the space she needed to close up the room. Maybe that was all she had ever needed. . .space.

❧

Katie pulled off her jacket before entering the restaurant. The white blouse underneath was free of coffee stains. Besides, she felt constricted in the jacket, especially on a warm June evening like this.

Karl met her at the door of her car, a smile lighting his face. "Are you hungry?"

"Always."

"That's the girl I remember."

Katie couldn't help but laugh as their eyes met. Just as quickly, she stopped. No matter how comfortable she felt around Karl, she did not want to give him the wrong impression. She didn't want to give *any* man the wrong impression, for that matter.

They walked together toward the restaurant with Karl making stilted conversation about the weather. She played along, not sure what else to do. Likely once they got inside, the tough conversation would begin—the one she'd avoided for twelve years.

The hostess took their names and within minutes led the way to a table near the back of the room. Karl put his hand on the small of Katie's back and guided her through the crowd. His touch offered a sense of security. She'd almost forgotten how safe she felt around him. How protected.

After they had ordered their food, she could put off the inevitable no longer. "I have to get this out," she said, looking him in the eye. "I need to tell you how sorry I am that I left like I did." Katie noticed his eyes glistened with moisture as she continued. "I know you probably think it was because of you. Because I didn't want to—"

"To marry me."

She drew in a deep breath and gazed at the table. "I'll admit I wasn't ready to get married. I had so many things I wanted to do, so many places I wanted to go. I knew if I got married, those things would never happen."

"Not necessarily."

"Still, the chances were slim." She gazed into his eyes, hoping to make him understand. "The more time I've spent away from Paradise, the more I've come to realize—it wasn't *you* I ran away from. It was the lifestyle. The constraints. I'm convinced I was born for. . ."

"Bigger things?"

She sighed—partly out of relief at the fact that he understood and partly because she realized how pompous that sounded. "It seems so ugly when you say it like that," she said. "And so. . .worldly. I'm not a worldly girl, Karl. Not really. I still have a very strong faith, probably stronger than it was back then. I just wanted to think in broader terms, travel in wider circles."

"I understand."

"And I certainly wasn't hoping for bigger things in a husband. In fact"—she gave him a shrug—"I wasn't *hoping* for a husband at all. That was the problem. I wanted to get out and see things for myself. I wanted an opportunity to spread my wings and fly a little, to see what I could become on my own. Without—"

"A man holding you back."

Another sigh slipped out, but she didn't answer right away because the waitress appeared at their table with water glasses in hand.

"Not everyone is meant to marry," Katie offered, after the waitress left. "There were plenty of spinsters in our community, remember? They cared for other people's children and took in laundry to earn a living. That would never have suited me."

"You were never meant to be a spinster." He reached across the table to take her hand. "But I do get your point. I know what it feels like to be trapped, to think there's no way out."

"You do?"

"Yes." He paused and withdrew his hand, looking a bit uncomfortable all of a sudden. "It's possible you've already heard this, but about two years after you left, my parents were both killed in a fire."

Katie's eyes filled with tears right away. "I did hear, though it was some time after, and I'm so sorry." She didn't add that she'd tried to track him down after getting the news. Tried to send a card. But by then, he'd already moved away from Paradise.

Now his eyes filled with tears. "The house burned to the ground after being struck by lightning. I lost more than my parents that day. I lost. . .my whole life. My existence. My place in the community."

"What do you mean?"

He shrugged. "I'm an only child, as you know, and not a child, at that. But to rebuild after such a tragedy just felt. . . overwhelming. I can honestly say I've never felt more alone in my life." He paused for a moment then added, "Don't misunderstand me. I knew the Lord was with me. I felt His presence daily. But I guess I needed the reassurance of someone who could help guide me. Advise me."

A thousand things went through Katie's mind at once as she took note of the woeful look on his face. If she had stayed in Paradise and married Karl, they would have rebuilt the farm. . .together. He never would have faced those things alone.

"I heard you sold the farm to Ike Biden," she said.

"Yes." Karl's face lit in a smile. "Ike was always such a good friend. He built a fine home on it, one now filled with half a dozen children and a wonderful wife. And I moved on to Harrisburg."

"Harrisburg?" She took a sip of water and then leaned back in her chair.

Karl nodded. "I had an uncle there. My father's brother. He convinced me I had what it took to become an attorney."

Katie's eyes widened. "An attorney? But the Amish are opposed to that occupation, aren't they?"

"My uncle was an Englisher. And it didn't take him long to convince me that I could actually do some good if I got the proper training. So, he pointed me in the right direction. I got my GED. My test scores were really high, actually."

"Same here." She couldn't help but smile. "Guess that small classroom environment really paid off."

"Yeah." He smiled. "After that, I went to college then on to law school."

"Turning you into a lawyer makes perfect sense to me." Katie chuckled. "You were always great at debating me on every little thing."

Karl laughed. "I can debate with the best of them, I guess. Least, that's what my uncle said. So off to law school I went. After I passed the bar, I worked at his firm in Harrisburg. Then, about a year ago, I was offered an opportunity to practice real estate law in Doylestown. I couldn't turn it down."

"I see." She paused and gave him an admiring look. "You've really made something of yourself, Karl. I'm so proud of you."

He shook his head. "There's a part of me that wishes I could go back. This new life is so. . .crazy. Hectic. Sometimes I miss the old days, working with my hands, sitting out by the creek with a fishing pole in my hands. It's different now."

"No kidding."

"What about you?" he asked. "Did you go to college?"

Katie released a sigh. "My story is a little different. For all of my bravery—slipping out of that window and running away—I have to admit I was pretty scared. . .of everything. I can't tell you how many times I wanted to run back home those first couple of years. But, instead, I stayed with Hannah. Listened to her talk about her dream of becoming a Realtor. She really had the real estate bug."

"She's a broker now, right?" he asked.

"Yes." Katie grinned. "But it took awhile. She wanted a home, a family, and a job. Doing all of that takes a lot of work."

"I'm sure she had a lot of help from you." Karl gave her a warm smile.

Katie shrugged. "Helping out with the kids—once they started coming along—was easier than facing the real world. But somewhere along the way I overcame my fears. Went to junior college for a couple of years. Got my associate's degree. Then"—she paused, remembering—"I guess it was watching Hannah that did it. She'd get so excited about the houses she'd sold. It wasn't just the money. . .it was the whole thing. Realizing she could balance a job and a family." Katie shrugged. "She's the true modern-day woman. Sort of the polar opposite of the ideal wife and mother we grew up with."

"And you wanted to be like that?"

"Well, I wanted to try my hand at a career, and Hannah was willing to walk me through the process," Katie explained. "I took the classes, got my license, and she set me up at Bucks County Realty." She looked over at Karl with a shrug. "The rest, as they say, is history."

The waitress made her appearance with their food, and Karl offered to pray. As they bowed their heads, Katie heard the same passion in his voice for the Lord that she had loved as a youngster. Surely leaving the Amish country hadn't diminished his faith. If anything, it seemed stronger now than ever.

As they began to eat, Karl dove into a discussion of particular interest to Katie, one near to her heart, in fact.

"Practicing real estate law has really opened my eyes to some of the atrocities taking place in the industry," he said. "I've never seen so many get-rich-quick schemes in my life. And I can't tell you how many clients have been taken advantage of—both buyers and sellers."

"I hear you," Katie concurred. "I've seen more than a few scams since I started in this business myself. Everything from overpricing houses to mortgage fraud. It's shameful."

Karl nodded. "I've seen a lot of other things that break my heart, too. Like all of the farms being bought up right and left by people who have no interest in the land itself. They just see it as a potential apartment complex or strip mall."

Katie's eyes grew wide as she listened. How interesting that their feelings were so similar, and on such a sensitive subject. "I feel the same. It seems like every day some investor sweeps in and buys up farmland, turning it into a parking lot or shopping center."

"I'm doing what I can to prevent that."

He spent the next fifteen minutes explaining his plan of action to save the farms in the area, and Katie listened with genuine interest. So. . .his love for the land hadn't died after all. In fact, he seemed more passionate about it than ever.

His faith had grown.

His love for the land had grown.

His desire to do the right thing had grown.

Clearly, Karl had entered the world of the English without letting it consume him. He was living proof that one could be in the world but not of it.

As she nibbled at her salad, troubling thoughts rolled through Katie's mind, and she had to wonder, despite her earlier comments to the contrary, could the same thing be said of her?

four

The following morning, Katie received a telephone call that shook her to the core. Her mother's tremulous voice conveyed the bad news. Her father had suffered a massive heart attack. He refused to be taken to the hospital. Would Katie come home right away?

She flew into action, packing a small bag and then telephoning Hannah. "I don't know how long I'll be," she explained. "But I want to stay as long as they need me. And it must be bad, Hannah. Otherwise, Mamm would never have used the telephone."

Hannah cried. Something she rarely did these days. "Tell your parents I love them and I'm praying. And tell my mamm. . ." Her voice trailed off.

Katie finished the sentence for her. "I will tell her that you love her and miss her."

"Thank you."

She made another quick call—this one to Aimee. Though she hated to think about business on a day like today, she needed to make sure someone took her calls and covered any potential showings. Saturday was a busy day for Realtors, after all.

Aimee listened to her explanation then responded with deep concern in her voice. "I'm here for you, Katie. Anything you need. And I'm praying for your father."

Katie pushed back the lump in her throat as she thanked her for being such a good friend. Then she ended the call.

The journey to Paradise was made with only the sound of a worship CD playing in the background. Katie offered up prayer after prayer for her father, pleading with the Lord to spare his life. Surely he would recover and go on to live many more healthy years. Right?

She contemplated many things as she wound through the familiar back roads of Lancaster County. Her father's condition. The sound of fear in her mother's voice. The fact that she'd only been home a handful of times over the years. Oh, her family had always welcomed her back with open arms, but she felt like an outsider every time. It seemed the trips back to Paradise were fewer and further between. Staying away was just. . .easier. A shiver ran up her spine as she contemplated today's trip. Surely it would cause her two worlds to collide once again. Was she ready for the collision?

Katie's thoughts drifted to her older brothers, Daniel and Amos. They were both happily married with children. As was often the case in Amish households, they had built their homes on the Walken property to be close to the family.

Katie smiled as she thought about her younger sisters, Emily and Sara. They were both married, as well, and Sara was expecting a baby in a few short weeks. Of course, the girls and their husbands lived inside the main house with Mamm and Datt. What would *that* be like—to be a newlywed living in your parents' home?

More curious still, what would it be like for Katie to spend quality time with all of her family members again, and under such sad circumstances? Would they still feel connected, even after all this time—and distance?

Her sisters' days were filled with washing clothes, sewing, scrubbing floors, cooking, and other such household chores. Hers were filled with clients, meetings, and bidding wars.

Her sisters knew nothing about the crazy, fast-paced world of real estate. Would they have anything in common at all, or would their conversations be strained, painful?

Thinking of the stark contrast between the two worlds reminded her of Karl and the conversation they had shared last night over dinner. She contemplated his apparent love for the Lord and his ability to live in the world without letting it consume him. And, after a bit of thought, she decided the same could be said of her.

I'm doing a pretty good job with that, too, she reasoned. After all, her love for material things hadn't gone too far. Sure, she loved great clothes. And having nice things in her office was a given. She had clients to impress, after all. But, as for letting her possessions mean too much to her, had she reached that point? She hoped not. She *prayed* not.

The appearance of a farm market and several small road-side stands let Katie know she would soon be home. She glanced down at the speedometer and slowed her pace as she drew near.

Off in the distance, a particular piece of property nearly took her breath away. The lush rolling pastures—greener than she remembered—seemed to be endless, and the white wood-framed farmhouse had a familiar feel to it. However, the FOR SALE sign out front told a different story. How sad to think the owners would have to leave such a lovely piece of land.

On the other hand, how wonderful for the Realtor to list an amazing property.

Katie was reminded at once of her recent lakefront listing and offered up a quick prayer that it would sell for the best possible price. Still, pretty as it was, it could hardly compare with the breathtaking beauty of Lancaster County's Amish farmland.

As she took it all in, Katie couldn't help but see the glaring irony. What were all of her possessions in comparison to the beauty of God's creation? Had she really traded this for a condo in the city? Sure, she'd filled it with great furnishings and artwork, but nothing would ever compare to the simple beauty found here, in the very place where she had started.

Odd, now that she thought about it. All of those years living in this breathtaking place, and she had missed the beauty all around her. Now she had replaced it with other things—also beautiful—but in a different way.

Hmm. Maybe her possessions had grown to mean too much to her, despite her earlier thoughts on the matter.

As Katie drew near her parents' home, she took a few moments to pray. Maybe, in the midst of the chaos and the busyness, she had set her sights on more worldly things. Getting her priorities straight might be in line, after all. She asked the Lord to forgive her and to redirect her thinking. *Take me back to the place where I don't care so much what people think—about how I look, what I own, where I work.*

Katie arrived at the farm around noon, her thoughts shifting at once to her father. As she contemplated his heart issues, she couldn't help but offer up another prayer on his behalf.

Pulling her car into the driveway felt odd. Of course, she had driven up the driveway many times as a teen—in a buggy. Often with Karl at her side. But only a few times in her adult life had she returned to the scene of the crime, the place where she had stolen away. Her gaze shifted at once to the window—the corridor she had slipped through into another life.

A shiver ran down her spine as she thought back to that cool summer night. The moon had been full, casting a more-than-adequate amount of light on the area outside her bedroom window. She had taken a small bag—not much bigger than the one she carried today. After easing the window open, she had tossed the bag out first then climbed through the small opening and out onto the lawn.

A trip to town on foot had proven difficult, in spite of the moonlight. She'd hidden out behind the store, knowing the place well and feeling safe there. When the sun had risen, she'd slipped into a telephone booth to make the collect call to Hannah. Her cousin had agreed to come and fetch her but insisted she leave a letter for her parents. Katie had mailed it that same morning.

Oh, but how she had missed her parents and her brothers and sisters those first few days. How she wanted to turn around and run right back to the safety of their arms. To the farm, the only life she'd ever known.

And now, as she eased her way from the driver's seat, as she made her way toward the front porch of the house where she'd grown up, Katie longed, once again, to run into the safety of her father's arms. Overwhelming guilt took hold, and she almost stopped in her tracks. Would she ever be able to do that again?

A few more moments of reflection might very well have sent her running in the opposite direction, but ironically, she was distracted by a golden retriever leaping up to greet her and licking her in the face.

"You must be a new one." Katie gave the pup a scratch behind the ears.

Just then, the front door of the house opened and her mother came running toward her. "Katie, oh, Katie!"

Mamm shooed the dog away then stopped short, possibly confused by Katie's appearance. After all, she had changed a lot since the last visit. A new haircut. A change in wardrobe.

A different approach to makeup. Yes, she continued to morph into quite the city girl, no denying that.

"Mamm." Katie wrapped her arms around her mother and gave her a warm hug. "How is he?"

Her mother shook her head and her eyes watered. "Not good. The doctor just left. He says it's in the Lord's hands."

"And Datt refuses to go to the hospital?"

"Yes. He wishes to be here, with his family. We cannot change his mind."

"The boys?"

"Your brothers are working in the fields today. We will send for them if we need them."

"Emily and Sara?"

"They have stayed close to the house, though Emily has just taken the buggy to town to fetch some items from the store. Sara is resting. This has been difficult on her."

Katie swallowed hard at that last comment. Had she been here, perhaps her sister's load would have been lifted. Once inside the house, Katie greeted her younger sister with a smile. Sara glowed with maternal happiness, and her extended belly showed that her time would not be long.

"You look wonderful," Katie gushed.

Sara put her hand on her stomach and shook her head. "Hardly. But thank you."

They embraced in a warm hug, and then Katie turned her attentions to the reason for her visit. After a few more brief questions about her father's condition, she drew in a deep breath and followed her mother to the bedroom.

There she found her father lying still in the bed. "Datt?"

"Katie?" His eyes fluttered open, and his trembling hand reached for hers. She sat on the edge of the bed, doing all she could to prevent the tears as she wrapped her healthy hand around his frail one. Oh, how the tables had turned. How many times had he reached for her with strong hands, held her safe?

What could she offer him in exchange?

※

Karl paced the living room of his small house and prayed. All afternoon he had waited for word about the Chandler place. His original offer had been countered by the owners. He offered a bit more, in the hopes that they would accept quickly.

Surely Aimee should know something by now. He picked up his cell phone and punched in her number. She answered on the third ring.

"No word yet, Karl." Her opening line drew a sigh out of him.

"Let me know the minute you hear something?"

"I will." She laughed. "If I didn't know better, I would think you were anxious about this one."

"Not anxious, really," he said. "I've just heard rumors that other investors have been looking to build a new subdivision out there, and I'd hate to see that. The property is some of the best farmland in the area and could be productive with the right owner."

"Are you a farmer, Mr. Borg?" Aimee asked.

Karl paused a moment before answering. "I used to be. But I'm not buying the property for myself. I have a list of clients who are interested in keeping Pennsylvania farmlands alive and well."

Aimee conveyed her satisfaction at his answer then shifted the conversation. "Before I let you go," she said, "I heard from Katie awhile ago. Her father is very ill."

"Oh?" The news startled Karl. He had only known Katie's

father to be a healthy, sturdy man—one in love with the land and with his family.

"Yes. Apparently he had a heart attack, and the prognosis is pretty grim."

"That's awful." Karl felt the pain acutely. Mr. Walken had treated him like a son, after all. "Thank you so much for telling me. I'll give her a call right away."

Without so much as a pause, Karl pulled Katie's business card from his wallet and dialed her cell number. She answered on the third ring.

"Katie?"

"Karl, is that you?"

He heard the catch in her voice and knew she'd been crying. "Yes, it's me. I just talked to Aimee. How is your father?"

"Oh, Karl, he's not good at all. The doctor has been here off and on all day because Datt won't go to the hospital. He says he wants to be here, with his family. But his heart is so weak, and Doc Yoder says he might not have long."

"I'm glad you're there. He needs you now, Katie."

"But. . .I need him, too." She began to cry in earnest now. "I don't know what I'd do if he. . ."

"I'll be praying," Karl said. "And I'll put in a call to my church so that others will be praying, too. In the meantime, I wonder how you would feel if I came out there. I could spend the night at Ike Biden's place. I think he would have me."

"You would do that?" Katie asked. "Drive all the way out here?"

"Your father has always been so wonderful to me," Karl said. "And I want to be there for him." He swallowed hard and added, "And for you."

Her quiet "Thank you" warmed his heart.

"I should be there by nightfall." He hung up the phone and threw some clothes in a bag, then settled into his car for the ride, praying all the way.

Going back to Paradise wouldn't be easy—not after all he'd been through. But going back, at least for now, certainly felt like the right thing to do.

five

Katie spent the first night at her parents' house at her father's bedside. She didn't want to leave him, even for a moment. He had rarely awakened since her arrival, though at times his eyelids fluttered and his lips would move as he recognized her voice. His breathing remained labored throughout the night, giving her great cause for concern. According to Doc Yoder, her father's heart and lungs were slowly shutting down.

If only she could talk Datt into going to the hospital, perhaps the doctors could do something to help him. But he would not be persuaded. Katie knew his decision to remain at home had nothing to do with rules and regulations. The Amish had no problem receiving medical care. No, her father's logic came from someplace else. She could sense it as the hours wore on. He knew his time was near.

And she knew it, too.

Many times Katie had heard people speak of death, how they could sense it in a room. She could almost taste it in the air, here in her parents' bedroom, but it did not frighten her. On the contrary, she found herself surprised at its gentleness. A lulling of sorts took over—like a mother rocking a child to sleep. Was this how God called His children home? Did He woo them with His love, urging them to let go of their pain and suffering and ease their way into His arms? Was death, like so many other things in life, a matter of releasing hold and giving God total control?

Katie vacillated between praying for her father's healing

and giving in to what appeared to be inevitable. Her heart ached at the idea of releasing him. She hadn't spent enough time with Datt, and now she regretted it as never before. Her days had been consumed with work, busyness. Why hadn't she come home more? Why hadn't she taken the time to sit and talk with her father more frequently, as she'd done so many years ago?

As the hours passed, regret gave way to exhaustion. Katie finally managed to doze in the rocking chair, though fitful dreams took hold—images from the past merged with scenes from her current life.

All too soon, the early morning sun peeked through the bedroom curtains, rousing her from her agitated slumber. She rose from the chair and approached the bedside.

"Datt?" She leaned down to give him a gentle kiss on the cheek. "It's morning."

He seemed to come awake, at least to some extent. His lips began to move, and she eased her way closer in to better hear what he had to say.

His words were strained and difficult to understand. "I. . . I'm so glad you've come h–home, Katydid. It. . .means the world to me."

A lump rose in her throat as he called her by the pet name she hadn't heard in years.

"I'm happy to be here," she managed. "I love you, Datt, and I'm praying for you." She gave his hand a little squeeze.

"I've prayed for you, as well." He spoke in a strained whisper. "I need to know. . .that all is well with you."

Katie gripped his hand, understanding his full meaning. "I am well, Datt, in every respect. I have a strong faith in God. Stronger than ever. I want you to rest assured of that. But please get some rest. We want you to get better."

"My focus is not on this world, Katydid. It is on the next." His eyes drifted shut, and she could almost see him slipping away into a dreamland, where heaven opened its doors to him and bade him come inside. His breathing grew more labored, and he drifted back off to sleep.

She leaned down to kiss him on his whiskery cheek. As she did, her mother entered the room, her face pale and drawn.

"Has he wakened?" she asked, drawing near.

"For a moment." Katie looked into her mother's tired eyes. "Mamm, you need to sit down. You look exhausted."

"I am fine."

"You've been up all night."

Her mother's treks in and out of the room through the night had been many. Katie knew Mamm had spent much of the night tending not just to her husband but to the needs of the others in the house. Nothing had changed there. Her mother had always put everyone else first, even in the hardest of times.

"I slept for a couple of hours on the sofa," her mother said.

"Aunt Emma said she would come back this morning. She will take over the household chores for you. Please rest."

Brushing the tears aside, Katie stood and walked toward her mother. She eased into the comfort of those familiar arms and began to weep. After a moment or two, her mother joined in, and before long, a quiet chorus of grief filled the room.

❧

Karl arrived at the Walken farm around eight in the morning, praying he was not too late. A fitful night's sleep at the Bidens' had left him feeling exhausted, but he chose to come anyway. Hopefully, they would be happy to see him.

As he made his way up the front steps of the house and

onto the porch, he reflected back on the hundreds of times he'd been here before. As a teen, he had arrived—a clean-shaven boy with butterflies in his stomach—to see Katie. To spend time with the girl he would one day marry.

Today, as he approached the front door, a different feeling washed over him. Karl knew that this visit would be far more somber. In fact, he couldn't help but feel it would change his life forever.

No sooner had the idea settled in his spirit than a large dog leaped up to greet him, placing its muddy paws on his chest and covering his face with slobbery kisses. Karl managed to get the mongrel under control, even managed to get him to sit obediently at his feet.

He gave the front door a gentle rap, then stepped back and waited. The door swung wide and a beautiful young woman greeted him, one who looked remarkably like Katie had in her late teens. This girl wore the traditional Amish garb, though it appeared to stretch over an extended belly. It took a moment to register. Ah. This must be. . . "Sara." He smiled and extended his hand.

She stepped out onto the porch, her face lighting into a smile. "Karl Borg! It's been so long." She gave his hand a squeeze and ushered him into the house. "Katie told us you were coming. We're so glad to have you."

"I'm happy to be here."

"Come and see the others."

Once inside, the other family members greeted him, and all concerns about how they would receive him were pushed aside. Karl recognized Daniel and Amos, Katie's older brothers. And Emily, the youngest of the Walken girls. But he had never met the spouses and children, and they were many.

After making introductions, Sara slipped off to fetch Katie.

He hated to disturb her, especially if she was spending time with her father.

As soon as she entered the living room, Karl could tell Katie had barely slept. Her eyes had a hollowed-out look to them, and what he guessed had once been near-perfect makeup was now smudged and faded. He wanted to sweep her into his arms, to tell her everything would be all right. Strange how his first desire was to protect her. That hadn't changed, in spite of everything.

"Karl." She approached with tears in her eyes, extending her hand. "I'm. . .we're so glad you could come."

He took her hand and gave it a squeeze. "I can think of no place I'd rather be than here." He glanced around the room. "With all of you."

At once, Mrs. Walken drew near and wrapped him in a warm embrace. "I know it will mean so much to Elam that you've come. Would you like to see him now?"

"If I may."

She led him into the bedroom, and he gazed in silence at the man whose head rested on the white pillowcase. Katie's father had aged considerably in the years Karl had been away, that much could not be denied. His beard, once salt-and-pepper in color, was a soft white now. His hair, once thick and dark, had thinned and lightened.

The thing that surprised Karl most, however, wasn't what he saw, but what he smelled. Though the room appeared to be spotless, an undeniable scent lingered all around him. He had heard of this before, of course, but never experienced it firsthand. Death had entered the room and had brought with it a compelling odor, one that almost made his head swim.

Karl reached over to take Katie's hand as she stepped into place beside him. He knew it would not be long. And, from the look on her face, she knew it, too.

Standing there, with Katie's hand in his, staring into the face of a man who had loved him as one of his own, Karl could not hold his emotion inside. He tried to swallow the lump that grew up in his throat, but it would not be squelched. Instead, he gripped Katie's hand a bit tighter, as if to say, "I am here for you. We will get through this."

She squeezed back, silent tears falling down her cheeks.

Standing hand in hand, they faced the inevitable. . . together.

six

An undeniable holiness permeated the room at the moment her father slipped into the arms of Jesus, an overpowering sensation Katie had never before experienced. She could genuinely feel the presence of God in a real and remarkable way. And yet, she had to admit, she could also feel the gut-wrenching pain of loss, a pain so deep that it seared her heart, cut her to the quick.

The moment her father's last breath was drawn, Katie wondered if she might ever be able to catch her own breath again. It didn't seem right—or fair—that she should be allowed to breathe. To carry on. That any of them should be allowed to carry on. How could they, when the man responsible for their existence had been taken from them?

And yet he hadn't been responsible, had he? Surely the Lord had been the one to give life to everyone in the room, and surely the Lord had seen fit to take her father home. And though she disagreed with both God's timing and method, Katie could not change the fact that her father's time on this earth had drawn to an end.

The mourning among those in the room took on varied forms. Katie's older brothers swooped in around her mother, making her their primary focus. Her younger sisters had privately confided their pain and grief but never openly. . . like this. Today, as they gathered around Datt's bed to say their good-byes, every broken heart risked exposure.

Katie's reverie did not last long, however. She watched in

awe as her mother began the necessary work related to his passing. *Always working, Mamm. Always working.* Even in a situation such as this, her labors never ended.

Her mother insisted on a few moments alone in the room to wash Datt's body before the undertaker arrived. Aunt Emma ushered the children off onto the front porch, where they sat together in near silence. Every now and again, someone would interject with a story about Datt, and then the tears would start again. Other than that, the only noise came from Buddy, the golden retriever, who let out an obligatory bark anytime someone came or went from the house.

Out of the corner of her eye, Katie watched Karl. He had been so good to come. And clearly, he belonged here. He really was like family, after all. Hadn't he always been?

Even now, in the midst of so much grief, Katie marveled at his ability to fit in so well with the other young men, to speak with them as if they were old friends. She appreciated his goodness to her family and would have to remember to tell him so later, when things were back to normal.

Normal.

She thought about the word with a sharp pain working its way through her heart. Would anything ever be normal again?

The funeral director, an older man named Mr. Slagel, arrived at the house within the hour, offering his condolences. He came in the familiar horse-drawn hearse, which Katie had seen many times during her childhood. She listened closely to all he had to say, though she knew, of course, what the next few hours and days would be like.

Her father would be taken to the funeral home and prepared for burial in a simple, basic coffin. Someone from the family would provide the lining, as was the custom in Amish households. Datt's body would be returned to the house in that same coffin, where it would remain until the day of the funeral. On the day before the service, friends and family members would come by to pay their last respects.

She had been down this road many times before, just never with someone in her own family. The whole thing seemed strangely surreal, as if it were happening to someone else. And yet it wasn't happening to someone else. This was very real. . .and horribly painful.

Mamm continued on, doing what she always did—working. She made arrangements for Datt's white pants, vest, and shirt to be sent with Mr. Slagel. Though Amish tradition dictated burying the deceased in white, Katie couldn't help but smile at the thought of her father in anything but the dark straight-cut suit he always wore. After years of seeing him working the fields in his traditional clothing, she wondered if he might be recognizable to her.

She paused for a moment to think about that. In spite of her haircut, makeup, and new clothes, Datt had recognized her the moment she walked in the room. He had sensed her presence even before his eyes had opened. Real love could clearly see beyond the external.

She spent the next few minutes pondering this, almost forgetting the goings-on inside the house. Only when several of the local men arrived to assist the undertaker did she shake herself back to reality.

A short time later, Katie stood off in the distance, watching with silent tears as Mr. Slagel and the minister lifted her father's body and carried it out to the hearse. The clip-clopping of the horses' hooves against the dirt-packed driveway provided a reminiscent sound, one she recognized from years of traveling by buggy.

But never had she watched a parent being led away in such fashion. And never had she anticipated the day she might.

Yet that day had come, whether she'd prepared for it or not.

After they left, she excused herself to the field behind the house, hoping for a time to release her emotions. Surely everyone would give her a bit of space without asking too many questions.

She eased her way through the crowd, noticing the questioning look in Karl's eyes. He seemed to ask, "Can I come with you?"

She did not respond. For now, she simply wanted time by herself. Time to mourn in private. Katie walked around the side of the house alone. Well, almost alone. Buddy insisted on joining her, his tail tucked between his legs as if sensing her pain.

Together they approached the back of the house. As her gaze landed on the beautiful green pasture behind the home, she was swept back to her younger years. How many times had she taken off running through the ribbons of green grass when her heart ached?

For a moment, she tried to convince herself that no proper young woman would do such a thing. But then, as the pain settled in and the grief took over, she kicked off her shoes and began to run. She made it past the doghouse and out into the clearing. On she ran, until her lungs cried out for relief. Katie could hear Buddy's pants as he moved alongside her. Funny how the rhythm of his steady gait kept her going.

She finally drew to a stop, breathing in great gulps of air. The tears came freely now, and the dog, perhaps in an attempt to bring comfort, lifted his front paws onto her chest. Katie gave him a rub behind the ears, and he nuzzled up against her.

She thought about Datt and all of the years she'd worked alongside him in the fields. She remembered the gleam in his eye as he'd taught her to drive a buggy. The look of sheer joy on his face as they sat across the dinner table from one another telling funny stories. Oh, how she wished she could go back, just once more. To have just five more minutes with him. Was that too much to ask?

After a period of true mourning, Katie finally dried her eyes. She looked back to see just how far she'd come and discovered the house was quite a distance away. This time, instead of running, she walked with slow, steady steps. Buddy, as always, kept his place beside her, a faithful companion. When she reached the back door, Katie dropped onto the porch step, exhausted.

She was greeted by Sara, who had a concerned look in her eyes. "Still running, Katie?"

"W—what?"

"I'm sorry." Sara bowed her head, cheeks turning red. "I didn't mean that the way it sounded. It's just that you were always so fast when you were a little girl, moving ahead out of the pack. Remember when we were young and you would challenge us to race from the front door to the street?"

"Oh yes. I thought you meant. . ." Katie's thoughts shifted back, once again, to the night she ran away from home.

Are you still running, Katie?

She took a seat on the porch step and tried to steady the trembling in her hands.

"I hate to bring this up," Sara said, taking a seat next to her. "But we need to let people know. Mamm has asked that someone write an obituary for the paper."

"Would Datt have wanted that?"

"He wouldn't want us gushing over him or making him

look better than others," Sara said, "but I think it's important to spread the word to others in the community. An obituary is not inappropriate."

"I see."

"Would you mind writing it, Katie? Your writing is the strongest in the family."

"I don't know if I can," she whispered.

Just then, Karl appeared at the door. "Do you ladies need anything?" he asked. "A glass of lemonade? Water?" He gave them a please-let-me-help look, and Katie smiled at his kindness. She shook her head, and he added, "May I join you?" with a tentative look in his eyes.

"Sure." Sara gestured for him to sit on the step next to them, and Karl eased his way down to a sitting position.

"We were just talking about the obituary," Sara explained. "I think Katie should write it."

Katie sighed, not saying anything for a moment. Then suddenly something occurred to her. "Wait a minute." She turned to look at Karl. "You were the best writer in our class."

"What?"

"Yes, and I'll bet you do a lot of writing in your line of work." She gave him an imploring look. "Would you help me, Karl? Please?"

❧

Karl looked into Katie's tear-filled eyes, and his heart felt as if it would come out of his chest. Of course he would help her. He would do whatever she needed.

Minutes later, with half the family crowded around him at the dining room table, he began the task of putting together a carefully constructed obituary, covering the most basic things about Elam Walken's life. He knew better than to praise the man, as this was frowned upon among the Amish.

No, plain and simple would do. *Just the facts, ma'am,* went through his head.

And so he listed the facts. On the surface they might appear rather ordinary—at least to those who didn't know Elam. Husband. Father. Church member. Farmer. Neighbor. But those who truly knew and loved the man would read between the lines. Elam's dedication to his wife and children was beyond compare. And his love for those in the community and the church could not be questioned. Best of all, his steady faith in the Lord resounded in every detail of his life. Karl did his best to insert these things in a subtler way.

After completing the piece, Sara insisted Karl read it aloud to everyone in the room. He did so hesitantly, hoping he'd done the man justice and yet hoping he hadn't gone too far. When he finished reading, tears filled every eye.

"You got it just right," Mrs. Walken said. She drew close and gave him a hug.

"Yes, you've done a wonderful job." Sara dabbed at her eyes.

The others in the family added their thoughts on the matter, all positive. Still, there was one who had not commented, and he longed to hear what she had to say. Karl looked into Katie's beautiful green eyes, wishing he could kiss away the tears he found there. He wanted to wrap her in his arms, to tell her everything would be okay. Instead, he waited in silence until she nodded and whispered, "It's beautiful, Karl."

He gave a simple nod in response then, realizing they couldn't fax the obituary to the local newspaper, offered to drive it into town and hand-deliver it.

Again, Katie looked at him with a look of genuine gratitude, mouthing a silent, "Thank you."

"Are you sure you don't mind?" Emily asked.

Karl rose to his feet. "Of course not." He would drive to town, no problem. In fact, he would willingly drive halfway across the country if he thought it would ease Katie's pain. With the piece of paper folded in his hand, Karl headed for the door.

seven

Katie marveled that the morning of her father's funeral turned out to be so sunny and bright. It hardly seemed fair, in light of the family's great loss. The sky overhead beckoned with a brilliant blue—the very color she'd avoided for years. She couldn't overlook the irony, no matter how hard she tried. Across the broad expanse of the back yard, wildflowers bloomed in colorful display, a vivid message that life, no matter how painful, would go on.

The unquestionable beauty of the surroundings kept Katie's tears at bay. As she stepped out onto the back porch, a gentle breeze wrapped her in its embrace, bringing comfort. Surely the Lord Himself leaned in to whisper in her ear as the winds drifted by.

She glanced down at her plain brown dress, one she had borrowed from Emily. She wore it both out of respect for her family and out of a desire not to draw attention to herself. With so many from the community in attendance, she simply wanted to blend in. This day was all about Datt, not an opportunity to make a fashion statement.

People from all over the county arrived by buggy for the simple service inside the Walken home, led by Jonas Stutzman, the local bishop. After everyone gathered in the living room—with some spilling out onto the porch—the bishop stood near the coffin to address the congregation. Katie knew that he would not speak of her father. Most Amish ministers did not mention the deceased at a funeral, choosing, instead, to speak from the story of creation.

"Earth to earth, ashes to ashes, dust to dust," Jonas read from his prayer book. "From dust man was created and to dust he returns—in sure and certain hope of the resurrection into eternal life."

He then spoke to the crowd from the Gospel of John, the fifth chapter, referring often to the resurrection of the dead. Katie closed her eyes and tried to picture it. The image of her father working in the fields came to mind, and in her daydream state, she could almost imagine him being snatched up, raised to the pale blue skies out of the green fields below to meet the Lord face-to-face.

She opened her eyes once again, trying to stay focused. Across the room, Karl stood with his old friend, Ike Biden. A feeling of peace enveloped her as she caught him looking her way. His actions over the past few days had more than proven one thing—his loyalty to her family had not wavered, in spite of her actions all those years ago.

In so many ways, Karl's loyalty reminded Katie of her father's steadfastness. Never had she met a man so dedicated to family as Datt, so selfless, so willing to give of himself to others, even at his own expense. She had never heard him complain. Not once. Her thoughts shifted to her work at the realty office. How many times a day did she whine about this little thing or that? Dozens likely.

If I could be half the person he was, I'd be doing well.

After the brief ceremony, the crowd of people shifted out-of-doors, to prepare for the ride to the cemetery. Each buggy received a number, designating the order in which it would proceed. Katie stood alongside her sisters, watching as Datt's coffin was placed in the hearse, a boxlike enclosed carriage drawn by a horse. Then she glanced down at the long line of buggies heading to the cemetery. They presented a solemn, impressive sight.

It took a considerable length of time to make it to the cemetery, what with the whole caravan of buggies, but Katie didn't mind. She wanted to put off the inevitable as long as possible. When they finally arrived, Karl appeared next to their carriage, ready to offer a hand to the women in the Walken family. He greeted her mother with a look of genuine caring and then helped Sara next. Finally, he reached out to take Katie's hand. She held on to his as she stepped down onto the ground—ground that would soon swallow up the wooden box that held her father's body.

Katie didn't realize that she still gripped Karl's hand until they arrived at the gravesite. With embarrassment taking hold, she loosened her grip and focused on the task ahead. She took one look at the chasm in the ground, however, and her heart lurched. If anything, she wanted to reach for Karl's arm once more, to steady herself. Instead, she brushed away a loose tear and planted her feet firmly on the ground, determined to remain strong for her mother and siblings.

As was the custom with Amish funerals, no songs were sung during the burial service. Instead, Bishop Stutzman read the words to an old familiar hymn as the pallbearers lowered the coffin into the grave. Afterward, the whole group silently prayed the Lord's Prayer. Katie thanked the Lord for the opportunity to close her eyes, to shut out the reality of what took place directly in front of her. She half wished the whole thing had been a dream, that she could open her eyes to discover Datt standing beside her, arm around her shoulder, offering comfort.

At some point during the prayer the tears came in force. Only then did she feel a hand slip into her own—a strong hand with a gentle touch. A hand with a tissue in it. She would have to remember to thank Karl later for his kindness.

Following the burial, friends and family members gathered around to console the family. Katie watched as her mother received embrace after embrace and tried to imagine what it would feel like to lose the only person you had ever loved. It surely left her mother's heart with a gaping hole inside, one only the Lord would be able to fill over the following months and years.

After the crowd thinned, Sara drew close for a quiet conversation. "Several of the ladies have brought food to the house, so we're going back for lunch." She looked over at Karl, who remained nearby, and added, "We hope you will join us."

"Of course." He nodded then looked at Katie, perhaps in an effort to get her opinion on the matter. She offered up a warm smile and a nod. Of course he could stay for lunch.

Having Karl here, beside her, felt so right, so normal.

Katie couldn't help but wonder, *Why did it feel so wrong all those years ago?*

a.

Karl kept a watchful eye on Katie throughout the afternoon. The exhaustion in her eyes grew more apparent with each step she took. In spite of his best attempts to slow her down, she insisted on scurrying around the room, tending to the needs of others. Working with great zeal, she filled plates and helped out in the kitchen. He couldn't get her to sit, no matter how hard he tried. In that respect, she was much like her mother. Perhaps too much.

Karl pondered that for a moment. The Amish work ethic had always been drilled into him, from childhood on. How many times while growing up had he heard the words "Be wary of idle hands"?

The Walken family members were the hardest workers in the community, and Katie appeared to have inherited a double dose of their energy. She never seemed to slow her pace, even during the hardest of times. He thought back to their childhoods, remembering the many times she had taken on extra chores around the farm, as if to prove she could outwork anyone else in the family. And then as a teen, her lengthy hours at the store had always concerned him.

Karl was reminded of his recent visit to her posh office at Bucks County Realty. Beneath the polished exterior, he'd noticed stacks of papers on her desk and a very full calendar with dozens of appointments penciled in. Surely she had taken on the challenge of hard work with a vengeance. No one could deny that. But when did she rest? She seemed to run full throttle day and night.

Running.

She'd been running for as long as he could remember, now that he thought about it. And if she didn't slow down soon, she would eventually burn herself out.

Unable to control the protective feelings that flooded over him as he watched her, Karl decided a change of focus was in order. He sat next to Amos, Katie's oldest brother, and engaged him in conversation. They talked about the future and the efforts Daniel and Amos would continue to put into the farm.

"We love this land," Amos explained. "And we will work hard to keep things going, as Datt taught us."

Karl knew the Walken farm remained in good hands but had to wonder how Elam's sons would manage without their father's expertise. The man had been a brilliant farmer, always producing the best crops in the county. And his dairy cows were among the heartiest, as well. Karl hoped Elam's sons and sons-in-law would take over where Elam had left off.

Later that afternoon, the crowd thinned and Karl finally managed to get Katie to himself. They sat together in adjoining wicker rockers, and she kicked off her shoes, grumbling about her aching feet. No doubt they ached. She'd been on them all day.

She closed her eyes for a minute or so, but when they opened, he noticed the glistening of tears. He longed to reach out and take her hand but didn't dare—not here in the house, anyway.

"You've had a hard day," he managed.

She nodded.

"Is there anything I can do?"

Katie let out a lingering sigh. "Not unless you have the ability to go back and change some of the mistakes I made in the past."

Karl smiled. "Trust me, if I could do that, I'd start with my own mistakes."

Her momentary silence bothered him, but not as much as what she said after. "You've never been prone to mistakes, Karl. I'm talking about the big stuff. The kinds of things I've done that hurt my family. And you."

He wanted to quote a Bible verse—to remind her that everyone sinned, everyone fell short of the glory of God—but didn't. Instead, he simply listened as she bared her soul.

"I know there's really no way to undo the past," Katie said with a wistful look in her eye. "I know that. But if I could, I'd go back and do so many things differently."

Karl wondered which things, specifically, she referred to but did not ask. "Life is filled with 'could haves' and 'would haves.'" He shrugged. "The only thing I can suggest is that you forgive yourself for the things you regret and thank God that every day is a brand-new beginning."

"Mmm-hmm." Katie took a nibble of coffee cake and then leaned back against her chair. After a few seconds of neither of them speaking, she finally broke the silence. "It's just hard to picture tomorrow as a new beginning after what we've been through." She shook her head. "I can't even imagine what my mother will do without Datt. And my brothers and sisters—they have so much work ahead of them with the farm, the house, the store. It's going to be a lot to handle without my father here to lead the way."

Ah. So she's worried about their workload. Feeling guilty about not being here to help. Somehow that didn't surprise him.

"What are you thinking?" he asked finally. "Are you contemplating coming back—to live?"

Her face paled. "Oh, Karl, I. . .I can't imagine it." Her voice lowered to a whisper. "Can you?"

He shook his head. "I've thought about it hundreds of times, but I truly feel the Lord has given me my marching orders. I don't think I'll ever go back to the Old Order again, to be honest."

"Me either." She shook her head. "But I won't be much help to my mother from Doylestown, will I?"

"I know you well enough to know you will stay in touch with her. And you can always visit," he said. "It's just a couple of hours, after all."

"True." She leaned back and closed her eyes once more, and he wondered if she might doze off. Instead, she whispered, "I never thought my dad would die. He just seemed. . ."

"Immortal?"

She nodded. "I know we're all going to die eventually, but I never really spent much time thinking about it, at least as it pertained to my family. And my dad, of all people! He was. . ."

"Invincible?"

She opened her eyes and gazed at him with a nod. "Yes. That's the word. He was the strongest man I've ever known. And he lived such a wonderful life."

Karl looked into her eyes, his heart swelling as he remembered something his father had always said. "Life is a gift," he said, repeating his datt's familiar words, "and death is a given."

"You're really wise," Katie said with a sigh. "Has anyone ever told you that?"

"Hardly." He laughed. "Though some of the attorneys in my office come to me for advice on occasion. And some of the kids in my youth group at church, as well."

"I can see why." She gave him a pensive look, and for a moment, he wanted to slip his arm over her shoulder, to draw her close.

Unfortunately, his cell phone chose that very moment to ring. He'd meant to silence it earlier in the day, out of respect for the family. Somehow, he must've forgotten. Thank goodness it hadn't rung during the service.

With a sigh, Karl glanced down at the number then reacted rather quickly to what he saw. "It's Aimee," he whispered, rising to his feet, "hopefully calling about the Chandler property. I'll take it out on the porch."

With a spring in his step, he bounded for the door.

eight

The morning after the funeral, Karl approached the Walken house with a fishing pole in his hand. The idea had come to him in the night. At first he had pushed it off, wondering if Katie would think it inappropriate. Then, after wrestling with the sheets for a couple of hours, he had settled on the idea that a visit to the Pequea Creek would be therapeutic for both of them.

Besides, he would be leaving for Doylestown later in the day to sign a final contract on the Chandler place. If everything went as planned, he would close on the property by month's end. A second call, this one from his office, had filled him in on a host of other work-related things that awaited him back at home.

Home. Hmm.

He sighed as he thought about it. As much as he wanted to get back to work, leaving Paradise seemed wrong, at least if Katie remained behind. Still, he could do little about it. Work called, and he must answer. If possible, he would spend his final hours here with her. Surely that would ease the pain of leaving.

Karl pondered that for a moment. Despite his best attempts, his heart still remained tied to Katie. Sure, he'd dated other girls over the years, tried to care about one or two of them in the same way he'd care for her. But nothing felt the same.

Why those age-old feelings returned with such a vengeance now, he could not say. After all, he had done his best to squelch them. Hadn't he? And surely she had shown no particular interest in him beyond friendship.

Thankfully, Katie answered the door. The weariness in her eyes stunned him.

"You could use a break." He lifted the pole for her to see. "What would you think about a little fishing trip?"

"Fishing trip?" She looked stunned. "I can't leave Mamm here alone with so much to be done."

"You go on, Katydid," her mother said, appearing behind her. "Aunt Emma is coming by to help me, and your brothers will be by later, as well. They will tend to whatever needs I have. Besides, I'm plenty tired. I might just lie down and take a nap this morning."

"Are you sure?"

"Yes." Her mother yawned then walked back into the house.

And so, in spite of her argument to the contrary, Katie agreed to join Karl along the banks of Pequea Creek for a morning of fishing, just like the old days. His heart swelled with joy at the thought of it. They would have one last morning together before. . .well, before normal life kicked in again.

As they walked along, Katie seemed preoccupied with their surroundings. "I can't believe these wildflowers." She pointed to a cluster of pink impatiens. "Were they always this colorful?"

"They were."

"And the grass." She pointed out across the pastures. "I honestly think it's greener since I left."

"Your leaving turned the grass greener?" He couldn't help but laugh. "That's pretty humorous, you have to admit."

"I'm just saying I don't remember things being this. . . beautiful. How was I raised in all of this without actually seeing it for what it was? The Amish country is the prettiest land I've ever seen, and I've traveled extensively over the years."

"Agreed," Karl said. "And I've thought about the irony many times."

"Irony?"

"We both left Paradise to enter the outside world."

"Ah"—she sighed—"I see what you mean. That is ironic, especially when you see how pretty it is."

They arrived at the edge of the creek, and Karl stood spellbound by the sight. Somehow he remembered the creek as being larger. Wider. But today it seemed a narrow slit across the land, just a trickle of water in comparison to the picture he'd locked in his memory.

In spite of this, he still wanted to fish, if for no other reason than to be with the woman who now captivated both his heart and his thoughts. He located the perfect spot for Katie to sit then joined her. After a few minutes spent baiting their hooks and tossing them out into the water, he felt compelled to finish the conversation they had started earlier.

"About what I said before—I didn't mean to imply that leaving the Amish life was a mistake," Karl said. "I don't think I could have stayed, in fact, and not just because of losing my parents. Still, something about being here in this part of Pennsylvania felt right." He leaned back against the trunk of the elm tree and tossed his fishing line into the water, adding, "Not just comfortable, either."

"It is serene here," Katie agreed. "Things are just more peaceful away from. . .well, the world."

Karl laughed. "It's interesting you should put it like that. I keep thinking about Adam and Eve in the Garden of Eden. They had everything they could've ever wanted right in front of them, and still they wanted more."

"I've thought about that myself. Several times, in fact. I suppose the same could be said of me, at a younger age anyway. Now that I've tasted and seen what the world has to offer, I'm not convinced it's all better."

"Yeah." He leaned back against the tree and listened to the rippling of the water against the rocks.

"Don't get me wrong," she said with a hint of laughter in her voice. "There are a lot of things I'd have a tough time doing without."

"Like?"

"Hmm." She paused for a moment. "Well, fast food, for one. And pedicures."

"Pedicures?"

She flashed an impish grin then shrugged. "Yeah. Once you've had one, it's impossible to turn back." After a moment's pause, she added, "I'd have the hardest time doing without my car. It's hard to imagine getting around Doylestown without it."

"Sometimes I wonder how we managed out here at all," he agreed. "Then I come back and I'm reminded of how simple, how peaceful life used to be."

For a moment, neither of them said anything. He closed his eyes and remembered back to a time when the two of them had sat together, listening to the same sounds, feeling the same early morning summer breeze. A time before either of them had owned a car or television or fancy clothes.

"What do you miss most about living here?" she asked.

"Hmm." He smiled. "I miss the sense of community. I mean, I go to a great church and I have a lot of great people around me, but it's not quite the same. People don't seem to have the same investment in one another. As children, we knew that people in our community would come rushing in if we needed something. Sometimes folks in churches get overlooked when they're going through troubled times. That always frustrates me."

"It is sad." She dipped her toes in the water and wiggled them around. "At my church they have committees for that sort of thing."

"Still, people are often passed over. We were never passed over as children, were we?"

"No," she said, "but I'm not naive enough to think I will ever have that same sense of family I experienced as a youngster. Not without moving back for good, I mean."

He shrugged. "You never know."

"What else do you miss?" she asked.

"I miss the barn raisings. And the buggy rides." He started laughing. "Remember that time we got stuck in the mud coming back from town? That older woman stopped to help us then offered us a ride back to your house in her car?"

"Mmm-hmm." Katie's eyes grew wide. "I remember how much I wanted to climb in that beautiful car and ride all the way back." A sigh escaped her lips. "Then I pictured the look on my mother's face if I'd come cruising up the driveway in a luxury sedan."

They both erupted in laughter, and Karl's heart seemed to come alive. Perhaps they weren't living in Paradise anymore. But sitting here, with Katie at his side, was the closest he'd come in years.

೩

Katie spent the better part of the morning trying to accomplish two things: catch a fish before Karl did and quiet the crazy beating in her heart every time he looked her way. For whatever reason, she felt like a jabbering schoolgirl whenever he tried to engage her in conversation. Only this time, her feelings were different than they had been as a teen. Stronger. Unavoidable, really.

Perhaps, as a young woman, she had managed to push aside any feelings for Karl in her quest to escape the lifestyle. But now, having tasted the things of the world, she suddenly found herself far more captivated by the gentleness of the man sitting next to her.

Surely the beauty of the Amish countryside wasn't the only thing she'd taken for granted as a child. Had Karl always been this good, this kind? And had she really not noticed how well their hands fit together? How beautifully they finished each other's sentences?

These things and more she pondered. . .until she felt a tug on her line. "Ooo! I've got one!"

She pulled up a smallmouth bass, and Karl whistled. "That's a beauty. Looks like someone's having fish for supper."

"Datt would've loved this." She sighed as she thought about the many times her father had fished alongside her and the gleam in his eye every time he hooked a prize catch.

Together, Katie and Karl worked to ease the frantic bass from the hook and into a bucket filled with creek water. She stared down at him in wonder, noting the beauty of his rich green color. He looked up at her with sad eyes, as if to say, "Release me, please."

In an impulsive decision, she lifted the bucket and carried it to the edge of the creek.

"What are you doing?" Karl gave her an incredulous look. "You just caught—"

He never had a chance to finish his sentence. Katie leaned down and tipped the bucket over, allowing the fish to slither back into the waters of Pequea Creek. She glanced over at

Karl with a shrug. "Sorry. I just didn't have it in me."

He stared at her in disbelief. She wanted to explain but wasn't sure where to begin. The little guy just wanted to be free. In many ways, she was reminded of herself as a teen, wanting to be released out of her tiny bucket—the Amish community—into a bigger stream. She had escaped from the bucket back then. Tipped it over herself and climbed out. But this poor bass needed help, needed someone to assist him.

Clearly, Karl didn't get it. He continued to stare at her with a look of genuine confusion on his face.

"I have a confession to make," Katie said, after sitting once again.

"A confession?" Karl wiped the perspiration from his brow and gave her an inquisitive look.

"Yeah." She brushed the dust from her hands. "When I slipped out of the window all those years ago, I made myself a promise."

"Oh?"

"Yeah. It might sound crazy, but. . .I've never worn blue since I left Lancaster County."

"Are you serious?"

A wave of relief washed over her as she told the story, one she'd never before told a soul, not even Hannah. "I grew up wearing mostly navy blue or brown dresses," she explained. "The night I slipped out of the window, I was wearing a blue one. My mother and Aunt Emma had just sewn it for me. For. . ."

"For our wedding day."

"Yes." She let her gaze shift to the ground. "It was the last time I ever wore blue."

"How in the world do you manage? Half my wardrobe is blue," Karl said.

"It would be a tragedy for you to avoid that color. Your eyes are the prettiest shade of blue I've ever seen." Katie clamped her hand over her mouth the minute the words were out, not quite believing she'd actually said such a thing out loud.

Karl laughed. "Well, thank you."

"To answer your question," Katie continued, "I do wear jeans. That's my only compromise. But no blue blouses or dresses, anything like that. I don't even own a blue night-gown." She laughed. "I can't believe no one has ever noticed I avoid the color."

"Probably because your eyes are green," Karl said with a wink. "You do wear green, I see." He gestured to her blouse.

"I do." Katie laughed and then remembered a story she wanted to tell. "When Hannah and Matt got married a few years after I moved to Doylestown, I was in quite a fix. She'd chosen blue for her bridesmaids' dresses."

"What did you do?"

"Convinced her that blue wasn't trendy. Talked her into lavender." She smiled, remembering. "She was fine with that, actually, so I didn't feel too bad. And I think she figured out what I was up to. She was raised alongside me, after all."

"That she was."

Just then a shout in the distance caught their attention. Katie looked up to discover Emily approaching, breathless and red-cheeked.

"You have to come back to the house," her sister managed between pants.

"What's happened?" Katie scrambled to her feet.

"It's Sara. The baby is coming."

"The b—baby?" Katie gave her sister a wide-eyed stare, hoping she didn't mean what she thought she meant. "But Sara's not due for four weeks."

"Someone needs to tell that to the baby."

"Jacob will take her to town in the buggy," Emily explained. "To the birthing center. But Sara is asking for you. She wants you there."

"The buggy?" Katie gave her younger sister a curious look. "Wouldn't it be better if I took them in my car?"

Emily shrugged. "We will let Sara determine that. She likely has enough time to get there in the buggy. But it's possible she will want one of you to call ahead to let the midwife know she's on her way. I would go myself, but Mamm isn't feeling well, and I think I should stay with her."

"Of course."

"Should I wait here?" Karl reached for his fishing pole.

Emily shook her head. "No, you should go, too. Jacob will need menfolk to gather around him, no doubt. Having you there will help keep him calm until the baby is born."

Katie gave Karl an imploring look. "Yes, please ride with me."

"I'll do one better than that," Karl said, rising to his feet. "I'll drive you there myself."

Relief washed over her as she nodded. How many times had he stepped in over the past few days, bringing comfort? Like an umbrella, he had shielded her from a multitude of storms.

And, from what she could tell, the rain was about to start up again.

nine

Karl eased his car out onto the road behind Jacob and Sara's buggy, ready to tail them all the way to town. He glanced at Katie, who appeared to be a nervous wreck.

"You okay?"

"Mmm-hmm." Just then Katie leaned over and pressed the horn. "Did you see that?" She pointed out to the road. "The guy in that SUV nearly hit Sara's buggy. If he had any idea there was a pregnant woman inside. . ."

She continued to rant as Karl watched her in amusement. In truth, the car hadn't come near the buggy at all, though he would certainly never say so. No, at this point it would be far better just to let sleeping dogs lie. Or. . .ranting women rant.

He felt like a snail crawling along behind the buggy. If only they'd been able to talk Sara and Jacob into joining them in the car; surely they would have been there by now. He'd seen the flash of panic in Jacob's eyes back in the house, but Sara insisted they would do just fine going to town in the usual way, reminding him that first babies rarely came quickly.

However, no more than a mile from the Walken home, the buggy came to an abrupt halt. Karl pulled his car off the road behind them and leaped from the seat to see what had happened. He found Jacob wide-eyed, seemingly frozen in place.

"Everything okay?" Karl asked.

Katie appeared on the other side of the rig, ready to be of

assistance to her sister.

Sara's eyes grew huge as she panted. "I. . .don't. . .think. . . I'm. . .going. . .to. . .make. . .it."

Katie took one look at Sara's face and made a pronouncement. "Everyone into the car. We're driving you the rest of the way."

"But the rig, the horses. . ." Jacob scrambled out of the buggy in a dither.

"Don't worry about them." Karl tossed his car keys to Katie, who caught them with ease. "Katie will drive you to town in my car, and I'll follow with the buggy."

"Are you sure?" Jacob had relief written all over his face.

"Of course. Now go on. Don't wait on me. No time to waste."

Karl waited until the car pulled out onto the road before climbing into the rig. Once inside, he took the reins in his hands and drew in a deep breath. He spoke a handful of words aloud, more to convince himself than the horses, "It's been awhile, boys, but I think I've still got it in me." With a snap of the reins, he was on his way.

The midday traffic breezed by. Several cars beeped their horns, trying to push him out of the way. Karl stayed as far to the right as possible but couldn't seem to calm the drivers down. The horses were a bit skittish, as well. Thankfully, he managed to keep them under control.

Just a mile or so outside of town, some tourists obviously took Karl for a true Amish man as the car slowed and one of them snapped his picture. No doubt they would get quite a jolt when they took a closer look at the photo and realized he wore jeans and a T-shirt. He wanted to shout, "Hey, cut that out!" but didn't. Most Englishers didn't realize the Amish frowned at picture taking. So Karl bit his lip and continued to plod along, easing his way down the highway toward the birthing center.

Only one problem. He had no idea where the birthing center was.

Ah, his cell phone. He did have that, though he'd kept it turned off since Aimee's call. Karl used one hand to hold the reins and another to punch in Katie's number. All the while, he couldn't help but laugh. What would the curious tourists think now if one snapped a photo of the Amish man with a cell phone in his hand?

❧

Katie paced the halls of the birthing center and prayed. From what the midwife had said, it wouldn't be long. Sara's water had broken while in the buggy, and the baby's appearance was imminent. There seemed to be some concern about Sara's blood pressure, which was running on the high side, so the midwife ushered Katie out of the room. Of course, there had also been the issue of the baby coming early.

With so many variables factored in, Katie had been instructed to wait in the hall—and to pray. And that's exactly what she did.

Until her cell phone rang.

She fumbled around in her purse for it, surprised to hear Karl's voice when she answered.

"Is everything okay?" she asked.

"Mmm, yeah. I'm just a little lost."

She proceeded to give him directions then conveyed her fears about her sister's condition. To her great relief, Karl offered to pray. She continued to pace the hall as his comforting voice took over. His appeal to the Almighty for a safe and healthy delivery of the baby eased her troubled mind.

As he finished with an "Amen," Katie was struck with the

realization that he'd telephoned her from inside the buggy. She tried to envision what he looked like, plodding through the center of town in the rig with a cell phone in hand, praying aloud as he went. Must be quite a sight, especially for curious onlookers.

Just about that time, she heard a cry from the other side of the door and realized the little darling had arrived. "We have a baby!"

Karl responded with a whoop, which nearly deafened her. "I have the birthing center in sight," he said. "I'll be there within minutes."

No sooner had he arrived than the midwife emerged from Sara's delivery room with a broad smile. "You can go inside now," she told them.

Katie took a step toward the door, but Karl's feet remained planted on the hall floor.

"You go ahead," he encouraged her.

She tiptoed into the room, her heart swelling with pride as she saw Sara sitting up in the bed with the little bundle in her arms. Her sister's hair hung down in long, beautiful tresses around her shoulders. Katie hardly recognized her without her kapp.

Sara gestured for her to draw near. "Come and see your niece."

"She's a. . .it's a girl?"

"Yes, and she wants to meet her aunt Katie."

Katie took a couple of tentative steps in her sister's direction. The little bundle in Sara's arms wiggled and let out a squeal. Glancing down, Katie noticed the squinted eyes and pink face. Wrapped up in a soft white blanket, she looked like a perfect little baby doll. Tiny, to be sure, but perfect.

"She's beautiful, Sara!" At once she wanted to scoop the

little darling in her arms but kept her distance, not wanting to intrude.

"Thank you." Sara looked up at Jacob with a warm smile. "I wouldn't have made it without him. He was such a help to me."

"I'm sure he was." Katie reached over to give him a hug. "Congratulations, Datt."

Even as the word was spoken, everyone in the room grew eerily silent. The truth registered at once. *"The Lord giveth and the Lord taketh away."* The scripture had never felt so personal, so. . .real.

"What will you call her?" Katie whispered, brushing away a tear.

With a smile, Sara gave her answer. "We've settled on Rachel." She gazed down at her daughter. "I think she looks like a Rachel, don't you?"

Katie peered down at the wriggly bundle. "I do."

"She's only five and a half pounds," Sara explained, "but we've been told she's healthy enough to take home."

"When?"

"By nightfall, I would imagine."

"Are you serious?" Katie could hardly believe it.

"Yes, we will give Sara a few hours to rest; then I will take her back to the house." Jacob looked toward the door with a curious look on his face. "That reminds me. . .did Karl make it here with the buggy?"

"He did." Katie resisted the urge to tell them about his adventures along the way. "He's just outside the door."

"Oh, invite him in." Sara gave an imploring look.

"Ah. . .are you sure?"

"Yes." Sara fussed with the covers to make herself more presentable.

It took a bit of wooing to get Karl into the room, but when he saw the baby, his face came alive at once. "Oh, Sara, she's amazing." He went into a lengthy discussion about her beautiful features, and Katie couldn't help but smile. The Amish weren't prone to accept flattery, but her sister didn't seem to mind the glowing report about her daughter.

After a brief visit with Karl, Sara nodded off to sleep. Jacob followed Katie and Karl out into the hallway. "It would be good if you could take the car and go back to the house to tell the others," he explained. "I'm sure Sara's mamm is anxious to hear the news, and Emily, too."

"Will you be okay if we leave?" Katie asked.

Jacob smiled. "We will be fine. And, as we said, we will return home by nightfall, anyway."

Katie sneaked back into the birthing room once more for a quick peek at her tiny niece. She reached down with her index finger and ran it along Rachel's cheek. "Happy birthday, baby girl," she whispered. "Now, sleep tight."

Minutes later, Katie settled into the car with Karl behind the wheel. She leaned her head back against the seat, trying to take in all of the day's events. For whatever reason, her eyes began to water.

"You okay?" Karl looked over at her in concern.

"Yes." She used a fingertip to brush away a tear. "I just find it interesting that the baby was born today, the day after we buried Datt. It's almost like the Lord wanted to prove that life would go on in spite of our pain."

"Amen." Karl reached to give her hand a squeeze, and they sat that way for some time.

"One life ends and another begins," she whispered. "Though"—the tears began in earnest—"I can't help but wonder what Datt would've thought of the baby. He was always so wonderful with the little ones."

"Your father was a man who really knew how to live—and love," Karl said. "I used to watch him with his animals and marvel at how he treated them with such tenderness."

"Yes." Katie smiled as the memories flooded over her.

"And I can remember one night when I was about seventeen," Karl continued, "your datt and I were standing out on your front porch looking at the sunset. I was ready to go back in the house as the sun dipped off to the west, but he wanted to linger a few minutes more. It might sound strange, but I learned a lot from him, how he paused to take in every precious second of a sunset. He told me to stop, to be patient. That I would miss the best part if I hurried away."

Before responding, Katie thought about the many times she had hurried away from things. And people. "What did you do?"

Karl chuckled. "I stood there, of course. And within minutes, the colors all kind of merged together—red, orange, gold, pink—they slipped away behind huge white clouds. It was like the outer edges of the clouds were suddenly broadcast in Technicolor display, like something you'd see in a rare photograph. And I almost missed it. But your datt—"

"He never missed a thing," Katie said thoughtfully. She paused as she pondered that, finally adding, "Until now."

Karl pulled his hand away and reached to start the car. "Oh, I don't know. I'd like to think he was looking on today, observing from above."

"Observing *which* part?" Katie turned to Karl and chuckled. "The part where his granddaughter entered the world or the part where a young man he once trusted enough to marry his daughter chatted on a cell phone while driving his buggy?"

Karl erupted in laughter as he slipped the car into gear.

"Okay, you've got me there. Maybe it's better to assume he was distracted getting the Walken family mansion ready instead of keeping an eye on us."

Katie thought about Karl's words all the way back to the house. It did bring her some comfort to know her father had led the way. Perhaps he'd already discovered a patch of farmland in heaven, ready to be plowed. Or maybe he'd stumbled upon a creek stocked full of smallmouth bass, ready to be caught.

At any rate, he was sure to be enjoying every sight, every sound.

Katie glanced out of the car window at the beautiful countryside and, with a wistful sigh, committed to do the same.

ten

Katie paid particular attention to the exquisite colors of the Pennsylvania sunset that night. Perhaps it had something to do with Karl's story about her father. Or maybe it had a little something to do with the fact that Karl pulled away from the farm at the very time the sun slipped off the edge of the horizon to the west.

Regardless, she stood quite still on the front porch of the house she'd grown up in and paid extra-special attention to the mesmerizing details as they unfolded, minute by minute. Sure enough, what started out as a blazing yellow ball in the sky eventually morphed into shimmering shades of orange and then fiery red. The whole thing seemed to happen in stages, and she didn't want to miss even one.

Funny. Watching the progression made her think of Karl—how her relationship with him had moved along in varying stages over the years, changing colors at each point. Her heart twisted a bit at the revelation. To know that she'd hurt him all those years ago brought such pain. And guilt.

Tonight, just before he pulled away, Katie had taken a few moments to beg for his forgiveness, something she should have done years ago. Karl, in his usual gracious way, had told her there was nothing to forgive, that God had already mended any wounds she might have inflicted, intentional or otherwise. Clearly, he had forgiven her years ago. And truly, the Lord had forgiven her as well. How many times had she poured out her heart, asking God to wash away any pain she might have caused her friends and family as a thrill-seeking young woman?

But now, as she stood staring at the sunset, Katie had to wonder, had she forgiven herself? If so, why did this gripping sensation grab hold of her every time she remembered what she'd done? Perhaps this would be just the time to take care of that.

As the red in the skies above faded to a soft bluish pink, Katie took a moment to release herself from the overwhelming guilt. To set herself free. Within seconds, the weight she'd been carrying began to lift, and she literally felt better. Now she could truly look to the future.

A sudden gust of wind whipped through the trees in the front yard, startling her. Katie discovered a hummingbird swooping down upon its feeder above, its tiny wings whirring with anticipation. Oh, to be that carefree! Did the little creature have a worry in the world?

After dipping his beak into the sweet liquid, the angelic creature flew away, apparently in a rush to move on. As he lifted off and disappeared from view, Katie's burden seemed to fly away with him, heading off to the vastness of the horizon. "As far as the east is from the west." She quoted the familiar scripture.

She thought about her relationship with her family and how like that little hummingbird she'd become over the years—touching down only when she felt like it. Her parents had sugared the water many times, trying to woo her back home. Still, she had remained distant.

Katie turned in curiosity as the hinges on the screen door let out a squeak. She smiled as her gaze landed on Emily, who appeared on the porch with a concerned look on her face.

"Ah, here you are. We've been looking for you. Mamm has made supper."

"She should be resting."

Emily shrugged. "Still, she's made supper and won't start until you join us. You know we never sit to eat until everyone is there."

Yes, Katie certainly knew the family's time-honored traditions.

She followed her sister into the house and joined the others at the table for what looked to be quite a feast. Surely her mother had not cooked all of this food today. No, much of it had to have come from women in the community.

As she took her seat at the table, Katie glanced over at her mother. Mamm's face carried a weary expression; the wrinkles around her eyes had deepened over the past few days. However, she never stopped working, not for a second. Katie wondered if her mother secretly longed for a different kind of life—one that would allow for an evening of Chinese takeout with an old movie on television afterward. If anyone deserved a rest, Mamm did.

Observing her surroundings, Katie had to admit her mother clearly liked things as they were. Everything in the home had a practical purpose. Each item had its use. If Mamm quietly longed for beautiful things—jewelry, clothes, and so forth—it certainly didn't show. Likely she'd never considered it.

These things Katie contemplated as she filled her plate with amazing foods—corn chowder, beef and noodles, cabbage, beets, and more. The smells wafted upward, tantalizing her, taking her back in time to when this kind of meal was commonplace. Diving into the familiar fare, Katie wondered if she would ever get used to her regular food routine again.

The conversation around the dinner table proved to be considerably quieter tonight. Her older brothers, she knew, were working up the courage to talk to Mamm about the work that needed to be done on the property. She'd heard them quietly talking earlier in the day, trying to iron out details. They had a good plan, but Katie secretly hoped they would pick another night to discuss such things. Tonight, all of them needed to rest both their bodies and their minds.

Thankfully, the meal passed quickly. As they nibbled at generous slices of shoofly pie afterward, the sound of Buddy's barking from outside the house startled them. Katie rose from the table and went into the living room, looking out the window to discover Sara and Jacob had returned in the buggy.

"They're home, Mamm!" Katie hollered out, and the room filled with people. They all waited at the front door until Jacob and Sara appeared, with the baby in her mother's arms.

"Let me see that little one." Mamm reached out her arms, and Sara willingly complied by handing the infant to her own mother.

Katie watched from a distance as her mother's silent tears flowed. She knew, of course, the thoughts that must be rolling through Mamm's head, the same words that had gone through her own, just hours before: *"The Lord giveth and the Lord taketh away."*

"This precious child is blessed of God," Mamm said as she gave the little one a tender kiss on the forehead. "And will follow Him all the days of her life."

A resounding "Amen" echoed around the room as their mother gave such an anointed blessing. Katie couldn't help but hear Datt's voice among the others. Surely he would have prayed over Rachel himself had he been here.

In her usual way, Mamm quickly handed the baby back to tend to her work. There were dishes to be done, after all, and floors to be swept. Idle hands were the devil's tools. Katie could practically hear the words rolling around in her mother's head, even now.

All pitched in, and before long they were able to enjoy a few moments together on the front porch. Katie gazed up into the sky, wondering if Karl had made it back to Doylestown okay. She wanted to call him, but several things prevented her from picking up the cell phone. To do so on her mother's front porch would be a direct insult, and. . .well, to call Karl so quickly after his leaving might make her look anxious.

Was she anxious?

Buddy came and sat at her feet, placing his head on her knees. Katie gave him a good rub behind the ears. "What are you looking for, sweet puppy—more attention?"

He nuzzled against her and let out a soft moan.

Emily chuckled. "He's just missing his wife, is all."

"His wife?"

"We have a beautiful female retriever in the barn. Looks just like him, only a bit smaller. Her name is Honey."

"I can't believe I haven't seen her running around," Katie said as she gave Buddy another affectionate rub.

"There's a reason for that. She's nursing eight puppies."

"Eight?" No wonder the poor thing hadn't been out for a visit.

"I'll take you to see them in the morning," Emily said with a yawn. "In the meantime, I think we're going to turn in for the night."

Katie watched as her sister and brother-in-law disappeared into the house, hand in hand. How wonderful it must be to have someone walk you through such a difficult time, to hold your hand and tell you everything was going to be all right. And how wonderful to know that same person would still be there, day after day, holding you close as you grew old together.

With a sigh on her lips, Katie resolved to shift her thoughts to something else, something a little less painful. She wondered how things were going at the office and promised herself she'd call Hannah in the morning before heading back to Doylestown.

Thinking of the realty office reminded Katie of the property she'd recently listed—the one near the lake. She hoped there had been some showings, despite her absence. She smiled as she thought about it. The lake. The house. The acreage. It was the closest thing to heaven she'd seen in a while.

On the other hand. . .as she glanced around the Walken farm as the evening skies kissed it good night, Katie was suddenly aware of the truth. No other piece of property on planet earth could begin to compare with the one in front of her right now.

☙

As Karl made the drive home, he remembered to turn his cell phone back on. Checking the messages, he noted four from the law office, including one that sounded fairly urgent. He would have to take care of that one quickly. He also found a message from Aimee at Bucks County Realty regarding the Chandler property. Finally, Karl was surprised to hear a somewhat lengthy message from a young woman at his church who worked in the children's ministry, asking if he would consider assisting in kid's church one Sunday morning a month.

As he flipped the phone shut, he took a moment to let that one sink in. Help with the children's ministry? He'd never worked with children before. Well, unless he counted all those years ago when he wasn't much more than a child himself. But even then, caring for little ones hadn't come naturally to him. On the other hand, just one glimpse at Jacob and Sara's newborn had melted him like butter. Maybe he had loved children all along and just didn't know it.

Still, he had to wonder about this particular young woman's request that he help out in the children's ministry. Karl had it on good authority—his best friend and pastor, Jay Ludlow— that DeeAnn Miller had her eye on him. And not just for ministry.

What any woman would see in him, Karl had no idea. For the most part, his workload kept him too busy for a relationship. And when he did think about spending time with a woman—which wasn't often—he had a hard time not comparing her to the only woman he'd ever loved.

Karl arrived back at his house, his stomach rumbling. *I'm going to miss the food from Paradise, that's for sure.* He reached into the refrigerator and pulled out a bottle of water and an apple. Settling down onto the sofa, he let his mind wander. For whatever reason, the only thing he could think about—the only *person* he could think about—was Katie. He wondered what she was doing right now at her mother's house. Had she turned in for the night?

He glanced at the clock. 8:45.

They were probably just winding down for the day. Maybe Sara and Jacob had arrived home with the baby.

In many ways, Karl envied Jacob. A caring wife. A healthy child. A beautiful home on some of the greenest land in all of Lancaster County. A simple life, and yet. . .

Life in the Amish country hadn't all been simple, had it?

No, after Katie had left, nothing had ever been simple again. In fact, the hole she'd left in his heart when she slipped out of the window had only grown larger over time. And when his parents died. . .

He remembered back to that day with a chill running down his spine. It had truly been the worst day of his life, one he did his best to put behind him.

Why now, after all these years, had it come back to haunt him? Likely, visiting Paradise had done that. And seeing the property now—with his own eyes—and how the land had been restored and a new home built only intensified the pain.

Karl pondered that for a moment, finally realizing the truth of it. He'd forgiven Katie for running away all those years ago. And strange as it might sound, he'd even forgiven his parents for leaving him behind as they'd ventured on to heaven ahead of him. The only One he might not have forgiven, now that he thought about it, was the One who could have prevented it all from happening in the first place.

The revelation nearly drove Karl to his knees. Had he been harboring unforgiveness. . .against God? Was such a thing really possible?

He settled onto the sofa to spend some time thinking through the matter. After a few minutes, he came to the conclusion that he had, albeit subconsciously, held the Lord responsible for the emptiness in his heart. With determination settling in, he opted to release that blame—once and for all.

eleven

There was something rather magical about an early summer morning on a Pennsylvania farm. Perhaps it could be blamed on the green leaves of the oak trees as the soft breeze moved them back and forth. Or maybe it had more to do with the misty dew on the grass, which put Katie in mind of those majestic summer mornings as a child.

The summers had been her favorite time, after all. How many times had she pulled off her shoes and run barefoot through the fields, hidden behind majestic stalks of wheat? And how many times had Datt come running after her, his resounding laughter riding along the breeze?

Now, as midsummer inched its way over her parents' farm, one thing remained abundantly clear—the seasons of Katie's life had changed. She could smell it in the air, like a much-anticipated rainstorm. She wasn't quite sure what it meant, but a shift was definitely coming. She could no more control it than she could summer turning to fall, or fall to winter.

Katie leaned back in her rocking chair, happy for a few additional minutes of solitude as the morning settled in around her. If only she could capture this feeling and bottle it! How wonderful it would be to take it back to the city.

The rhythmic creaking of the rockers against the aging wooden slats of the front porch lulled her into a dreamlike state. After a few carefree moments, however, the time came to say good-bye, not just to the morning but to the farm. And her family. And that precious new baby. She had to return home. Her work could wait no longer.

Less than an hour later, Katie loaded her suitcase into the back of her car. She paused to look up as she heard Emily's voice ring out. "Katie, before you leave, you have to come to the barn to see the puppies."

She closed the back door of the car and turned to her sister with a forced stern look. "Okay, but promise me you won't try to pawn one off on me. I don't have any room in my condo for a golden retriever, trust me." She couldn't even imagine such a thing, no matter how hard she tried.

"I promise." Emily grinned. "But they're the most precious little things. You've really got to see for yourself." She shifted into a lengthy discussion about the breed, focusing on their loyalty to owners and uncanny ability to adapt to life in a variety of settings. Katie tried not to respond, biting her tongue till it nearly bled. She would not be swept in, no matter how hard Emily tried.

Katie plodded along across the yard behind her sister until they drew near to the barn. Her heart ached as she stepped inside, remembering back to the day when friends from the community had come to help Datt raise the spacious white building. What fun they'd had helping Mamm and the other ladies prepare food and serve it to all the menfolk. The day had been joyous, from beginning to end.

Katie especially remembered Karl—the look of contentment on his face as she handed him a glass of lemonade. How his blue eyes had sparkled.

Why could she see so clearly now what she'd managed to overlook all those years ago?

Katie looked around the inside of the barn, noticing it seemed bigger than ever. . .and emptier than ever without Datt here to fill it with his love and laughter. He'd always managed to make work enjoyable. His fun-loving personality, larger than that of most men in their small community, had been his strength. And his weakness. Many had whispered in private that Elam Walken tried to draw attention to himself by making others laugh. Katie had always tightened her fists at such a suggestion.

Strange. She found her fists tightened now, too. Thankfully, the sound of whimpering pups off to her right offered a nice distraction from the bittersweet memories. Katie followed the sound until she stood directly in front of the mama dog and her puppies. The little darlings tussled about, pawing each other and yipping. The mama dog, God bless her, looked exhausted. Katie reached down to scratch her behind the ears. "You're a brave girl," she whispered.

Emily knelt down in the hay and bade Katie to do the same. She did so reluctantly, having already dressed for her trip back to Doylestown. It certainly wouldn't look very good to show up at the office with hay, and who knew what else, all over her knees.

Still, the puppies were awfully cute, and one in particular seemed to call out to her. She reached down to pick it up, cradling it close to her heart. Suddenly Katie's nice clothes didn't matter. The puppy nuzzled its cold black nose against her neck, and she giggled, breathing in that soft puppy scent she remembered from childhood.

"We call that one Miracle," Emily said. "She's the runt. We almost lost her at birth. I doubt anyone's going to want to buy her."

"Are you serious?" Katie pulled the pup back for a scrutinizing look. "Why not? She's gorgeous."

"Still, she's small. And very attached to her mama. She's just the kind to think she was born for indoor life, not outdoor."

Katie held the pup a second longer—until she realized what her sister was trying to do. "Oh no you don't," she said, putting the puppy back down. "You're not getting to me that easily."

"What?" Emily gave her an innocent look. "What did I do?"

"You know very well." Katie stood and brushed the hay from her knees. She looked down at her brown silk blouse and sighed as she saw the blond dog hair Miracle had left behind.

"Golden retrievers don't shed," Emily interjected.

"Sure they don't." Katie did her best to remove the hairs with her fingertips, but they clung stubbornly to the silk.

Emily rose to her feet and gave Katie the saddest look. "You're really leaving, aren't you?"

"Yes. Did you think. . .?"

Emily shrugged. "I've been hoping you would change your mind and stay here, with us." She gave a little pout.

Katie took her sister by the hand. "When I'm not here, I miss you so much. All of you. I hope you know that. And, in case you doubt it, I love you as much now as ever. I do wish I could see you more. I'm just so—"

"Busy."

"Yeah. But I promise I'll come back more often. I won't wait so long next time." She wanted to add, *And if you just had Internet access, I could stay in touch. I would write you every day. Send you funny e-mail forwards to make you laugh. Talk to you over Instant Messenger.*

Instead, she said nothing.

Katie gave the puppy another glance then looked at her watch. "I've got to go soon, but there's another baby I need to see first." In fact, she could hardly wait to hold Sara's little daughter in her arms one last time before making the drive back home.

Home. Hmm.

She quickly made her way out of the barn and across the property to the main house, where she found Sara helping Mamm with the canning in the spotless kitchen.

"Shouldn't you be resting?" Katie scolded as she washed her hands at the kitchen sink.

"I'm fine. Fit as a fiddle," her sister responded. "No point in pampering me just because I've had a baby."

"Still." Katie shook her head and decided not to argue, though she would certainly hope for a bit of pampering if she'd been the one to have the baby. Instead, she walked over to the cradle and reached down to scoop up her niece in her arms and rock her back and forth.

"I just got her to sleep!" Sara pretended to look irritated.

"I'll put her right back down. I promise." Katie gave Rachel a half dozen little kisses all over her wisps of hair and pink little cheeks. "Don't you miss your auntie too much, little girl," she whispered. "And you do everything your mamm tells you."

A twinge took hold of her heart as she said the word "Mamm." No matter how much she tried to convince herself otherwise, Katie longed to be a mother, too, to have a darling baby girl to call her own. She'd known it from the day Hannah's first child was born, though she'd pushed the feelings aside. But now, as she stared into this precious newborn's face, she could deny it no longer.

Katie placed the infant back down with a sigh, making sure she was wrapped snugly in the little blanket. Plain white, of course. No frills for this child. No ruffled bonnets or darling pink outfits. Nothing to draw attention to—or exaggerate— the baby's beauty. No, this little one would be raised with far simpler attire than most newborns these days.

"I don't think I could do it," Katie whispered. "I'd want to dress you up like the baby doll that you are!"

She looked over at her mother and sister as they worked alongside one another. They'd never known the thrill of dressing in fancy clothes, either, and had probably never missed it. No, they seemed more than content to keep things as they were. And to stay busy. Always busy.

Just watching her mother made Katie tired. Mamm had a quiet inner strength, born out of trusting God, even in the hardest of times. A strength that gave her the tenacity to keep going, keep working. This Katie knew from years of careful observation. Mamm would work her way through the pain and the grief and would do it out of love for her children and her God.

As Katie watched her family members working together, her heart ached. What would it be like to work side by side with those you loved, sharing nearly every moment together? Would you giggle over the sweet things and cry over the sad ones?

She thought at once of Hannah and the work they did together at the office. As much as she loved her cousin, it just didn't feel the same. Perhaps with a little effort it could. She would work on it, and things would improve.

For now, the inevitable was upon her. Katie moved in her mother's direction, arms extended. "I. . .I have to go, Mamm."

Her mother turned, brushing tears from her lashes. Katie could almost read the message in those weary eyes. They cried out, "We miss you, Katydid. Come back to us."

For a moment, she almost resisted. Then she remembered the workload awaiting her back at Bucks County Realty and knew she could hesitate no longer.

After a tearful good-bye, Katie climbed into her car and headed out on her way. She thought about that tiny hummingbird lighting down upon its feeder only to lift off and fly away once again, and a niggling feeling of guilt crept over her. How she wanted to dip her beak in that sweet water once more before taking flight.

Katie tried not to look back as she pulled away from the farm but couldn't resist. As her gaze fell on the barn, she thought once again of her datt, and the tears flowed freely. For the first several miles out of Paradise, she grieved the loss of her father. She'd never felt pain so deep.

Then, as her thoughts shifted, Katie cried because of that sweet little puppy, Miracle. Silly, she knew. But she couldn't stop the tears from flowing every time she remembered the feel of that little angel's fur against her neck and the scent of puppy breath against her cheek.

Katie finally managed to get things under control about the time she hit the turnpike. She tried to convince herself that her life, though chaotic and somewhat disconnected, fulfilled her on nearly every level.

And she did everything in her power to force that crazy image of the hummingbird out of her mind—once and for all.

◆

Karl hung up the phone after talking to his pastor and sighed. Sometimes he wished he'd chosen another profession, something simple like ditchdigging. Or brain surgery. Anything would be better than real estate law, at least today.

What was it with friends and relatives? Why did they feel that asking for free legal advice was okay? He'd dished out far too much of it over the years. And on a day like this, with so much already going on, he hardly had time for other people's problems. Right?

With a heavy heart, Karl quickly repented for his frustrations. He didn't really mind offering advice where his pastor was concerned. No, he would gladly share his expertise with Jay. Only one problem this time—his good friend appeared to be dealing with something complex, something that might not end well for the church unless Karl got involved personally. And, if he had to be completely honest about it, Karl didn't *want* to get involved personally.

For a moment he thought about Katie, how she'd climbed out of her bedroom window and run away from a seemingly unavoidable situation. Karl's gaze shifted across the room to the large window, and he had to laugh. As much as he'd like to avoid getting involved in the church's situation, climbing out of this window would be impossible. He was on the third floor, after all. Still the temptation did present an issue.

Karl yawned and stretched in an attempt to stay awake. Nothing seemed to help. Maybe a ten-minute power nap would help. He closed his eyes and reflected back on his time at Pequea Creek. He couldn't stop thinking about Katie—how she'd tossed that bass back into the water. Crazy. Still, there had been a look in her eyes, something he couldn't quite determine. Almost as if she'd understood the fish's plight. Didn't make a bit of sense to him, regardless.

He drifted off to sleep, and the dreams came in dizzying array. He fancied himself a fish, swimming upstream in Pequea Creek, trying to avoid being caught. Off in the distance he saw what appeared to be a slender, iridescent worm, slithering through the water. He opened his mouth to snag it, quickly discovering he'd been caught on a cleverly disguised hook.

He felt his body being pulled, pulled, pulled—out of the water and into the air. Gasping for breath, he stared directly into the wide green eyes of Katie Walken.

Even in his dreamlike state, Karl knew enough not to resist. However, he found himself devastated when she pulled him from the hook. . .

. . .and tossed him back into the water.

twelve

Katie arrived back in Doylestown late in the afternoon. She rushed to meet all of her appointments and return all of her phone calls, stunned at how much work had piled up. Thankfully, one of those calls was from a woman named Debbie Morrison, a California transplant wanting to look at the property Katie had just listed. The big one.

Katie whispered a prayer that tomorrow's showing would go well and that the Morrison family would fall in love with the place. And make an offer, of course. She quickly did the math. If they bought the house at the asking price—a million two—her commission would be seventy-two thousand dollars, more or less. Yes, she could certainly make do with that.

A thousand ideas swept through her mind at once. With that kind of money, she could make a hefty donation to her church and give a good deal of money to missions besides. She could send a check to Mamm monthly to help with expenses. Katie's mind reeled as she considered all of the possibilities. How she would love to bless her mother, especially now. Seventy-two thousand dollars would spread a long way.

Her thoughts shifted to the condo. For years, she'd wanted to renovate, to add wood floors throughout. That might be possible now. If she went with wood floors, she might be able to consider a small dog as a companion. Right?

With such grandiose plans in mind, Katie allowed her

thoughts to soar further. Maybe she could eventually update the appliances in the kitchen, something she'd wanted to do for years. The seal on the refrigerator had been giving her fits, and one of the knobs on the stove was broken. Wouldn't it be wonderful to replace them both with brand-new things?

Yes, there were a great many things she could do with funds of that magnitude. Again, Katie whispered a prayer for God's will to be done. She didn't want to get ahead of Him, by any stretch.

She finally made it home from the office about the time the sun fell past the horizon. Though she longed to look up in the sky and see the same beautiful colors she'd noticed back in Paradise, the high-rise across the street blocked her view. She stood in the parking lot a moment and closed her eyes, trying to remember last night's sunset.

Had it really only been twenty-four hours? Strange. It seemed she'd been back for ages. Perhaps this had something to do with the uncanny amount of work she'd accomplished in such a short time.

Katie opened her eyes and sighed, trying to make the best of things. She picked up her pace as she made her way into the condo. Once inside, she placed her laptop, cell phone, and purse on the kitchen counter and headed off to the bedroom to change into her most comfortable pj's.

Once settled, she looked in the fridge for something to eat. Nothing much grabbed her attention; likely eating at her mother's table once again had convinced her tastebuds they deserved more than the usual after-work fare. Regardless, she ended up reaching for a frozen dinner, something rather bland looking with pasta and chicken. She popped it in the microwave and leaned against the countertop to wait for the beep.

In the meantime, Katie opened her laptop, waiting a moment for it to boot up. By the time her food was ready to come out of the microwave, her high-speed wireless Internet access had kicked in and she scrolled through her e-mails to see if Karl had written. She knew he was busy—he'd said as much—but she still hoped he would write. Or call.

When Katie realized her e-mail box held nothing from him, she reached for her cell phone to check for missed calls. One from Hannah. Another from Aimee. Nothing else.

For whatever reason, her heart twisted at the idea that Karl hadn't tried to contact her yet. Why it mattered so much, she could not be sure. Until a week ago, she hadn't given him another thought. *Why do I feel like this? Why do I even care? Surely if he wanted to stay in touch, he would. Right?* Then again, maybe she had imagined the look in his eyes yesterday at the creek. Maybe the security of his hand in hers had been something she'd made too much of in her girlish daydreams.

Or maybe the busyness of his schedule prevented it for now. In the hours since she had arrived back in Doylestown, Katie had barely had time to catch up. Chaos reigned. Nothing new there. Perhaps Karl was dealing with the same thing on his end.

The microwave beeped again, and Katie reached to grab the instant meal. After pulling back the half-melted cover, the steam from the food inside burned her fingers. She almost dropped the hot plastic container but managed to get it under control. Then, she carried it to the table with the laptop carefully balanced in her other hand. Surely she could catch up on some work while she ate. Nothing wrong with that, right? After all, idle hands were the devil's tools.

Katie's thoughts wandered to her life as a teen, when her greatest exposure to the world had been the store where she waited on curious tourists. Things had changed considerably over the years. If she still lived in Paradise, she certainly wouldn't be using the Internet tonight.

On the other hand, if she still lived in Paradise, she'd probably be happily married to Karl Borg and have half a dozen kids by now. And a dog. They'd be eating fish for dinner—fish that she'd caught in Pequea Creek. And shoofly pie for dessert.

As she nibbled on the somewhat mushy pasta and flavorless chicken, an instant message came through. Katie smiled as she saw Karl's words:

"Are you there?"

"I'm here," she typed in response.

"I'm still at work."

"No way." She took another bite of her food, nearly burning her tongue. Katie wished she'd grabbed a diet soda out of the fridge before sitting down but didn't dare budge now. She didn't want to miss anything. "What are you working on?"

"Helping my church unwind itself from a legal mess."

"Whoa. Care to elaborate?"

"Maybe later," he sent. "Right now I'm worn out."

"Me too." She took another bite of her food and thumbed through the files she'd brought home from work. "But good things are happening on this end. I might have an opportunity to make a sale. A really big one."

"With a smile like yours, who wouldn't buy a house from you?"

A girlish giggle slipped out as Katie thought about his words. Looked like their issues from the past were truly behind them. Better yet, it looked like their present—and their future—was brighter than ever. Especially if he kept saying things like that.

If they could just manage to spend a little time together...

"I wish things would slow down," Karl sent. "I would ask you out to dinner."

Katie smiled as she responded. "I would accept."

"In that case...tomorrow night?"

"Sorry. I have a meeting." She took another nibble of her meal, realizing it tasted a bit more like school paste than pasta.

"Friday then?"

Katie sighed as she typed, "I promised Hannah I'd help with her daughter's birthday party."

"Looks like I'm never going to see you again."

As Katie stared at the screen, she realized just how painful it would be never to see him again. Perhaps the twinge she now felt was a small taste of what he had experienced the first few years after she left Paradise. Maybe she had it coming to her.

Or maybe God could use this opportunity to turn the tables.

"Want to come to a nine-year-old's pizza party?" she typed. Katie leaned back against her chair and waited. Likely he would think she was nuts.

She couldn't help but laugh when he responded with, "Pepperoni?"

"Sure. Whatever you like. Call me on Friday afternoon, and I'll give you the specifics. In the meantime, I'll be praying about your church situation."

"Thanks. And I'll be praying you make that big sale. Then you can take me out for a steak dinner to celebrate. With cheesecake for dessert."

"Mmm." *Nearly as good as shoofly pie.* "You've got a deal."

"G'night, Katie."

"G'night."

As she signed off, Katie leaned back in her chair and closed her eyes. Funny, even with them shut, she could still see Karl so clearly in her imagination. His sturdy build. His blond hair. Those amazing blue eyes. His heart for others.

"Thank You, Lord, for showing me what I missed years ago. And thank You—a hundred times over—for giving me a second chance. And now, Lord, a special request. . .please. . . help me not to blow it."

⁂

Karl tossed a load of laundry into the washing machine and poured in the detergent. As he did, he reminded himself to take his gray suit to the dry cleaners tomorrow morning, along with several dress shirts. For now, he was happy to wear shorts and a T-shirt—his usual after-work attire.

Closing the lid of the washer, he looked around the basement with a sigh. So many things needed to be done around the house, but he rarely had time. Still, he couldn't stand the idea of things being in disarray. Every night as he laid his head on the pillow, Karl promised himself: *Tomorrow. Tomorrow I'll get organized.*

Unfortunately, with his workload so high, tomorrow never seemed to come. Maybe one day he would hire one of those home organizers to come and help him put everything in its place. Someone who had an eye for such things and time to accomplish them.

Karl's thoughts shifted to the farm where he'd grown up. Everything was always in its place in his father's shed. Every tool taken care of. Every square inch of the house in perfect order at all times.

Karl sighed. Seemed that no matter how hard he worked, he could never keep up with things, though not for lack of trying.

Don't be so hard on yourself.

Where the words came from, he couldn't be sure. Had the Lord dropped them into his heart, or were they his own? Regardless, Karl made a quick decision to pay special attention to the message. As long as he gave every situation his best, he had no reason to scold himself for the things that remained undone, right?

And speaking of things that were undone. . .

He smiled as he thought back over his instant message with Katie. Their back and forth bantering had been fun, but he hated to read too much into it. Once before, he had given his heart to her only to be disappointed. Was she just toying with his emotions this time around, or had a spark really ignited between them?

Karl offered up a prayer, asking the Lord for a second chance. He dared to hope for what had once seemed impossible. And once again he opened his heart, making himself completely vulnerable.

Surely this time around nothing would go wrong.

He prayed.

As exhaustion set in, Karl was reminded of Katie's invitation to her niece's birthday party. He could hardly wait. And who knew? Maybe a pizza party with a bunch of nine-year-olds would be fun. He enjoyed being around kids. Certainly, getting to see Katie once again would make his day.

If only he could keep his heart in his chest from now till Friday, he would be just fine.

thirteen

The following day, Katie showed the million-dollar property to the Morrison family from Southern California. They were particularly drawn to the land around the house, and why not? Surely it was some of the prettiest in the county. Green rolling farmland beckoned, and the spacious yard was dotted with colorful flower beds. The house, a sprawling five-bedroom, proved to be more than big enough for their feisty brood of four children.

Katie fell in love with the youngsters right away, especially the tiniest girl, who, ironically, shared her new niece's name: Rachel. The youngster—probably no older than four or five—held Katie's hand as they wound their way through the many rooms of the house. The little girl oohed and aahed over many of the home's upgraded features, as did others in the family.

And who could blame them? The beautiful two-story, five-bedroom home sat on some of the prettiest acreage in Bucks County. And being this close to the lake was a plus, especially for a family used to living along the Pacific. Mr. Morrison told countless stories about his boat, and Mrs. Morrison raved over the spacious kitchen with its updated cabinets and granite countertops.

All the while, Katie kept her cool and answered their questions. She didn't want to do anything to sway them one way or the other. If the Lord intended them to have this house, they would have it. In the meantime, she would simply enjoy being with them. She could imagine herself a part of a family like this one day. A sprawling house. A handful of kids. A husband who talked about his boat.

Maybe. Someday.

A couple of hours later, she received the call. The Morrisons wanted the house. And the best news of all. . .she now represented both the buyer and the seller. That meant the full 6 percent commission.

Katie contacted the owner on his cell phone. He answered on the third ring.

"Mr. Hamilton?" She tried to contain her excitement so as not to give away the surprise.

"Yes?"

"Katie Walken from Bucks County Realty."

"Calling with good news, I hope."

"Very good news. We have an offer on the property—full asking price."

"Well, I want to move forward, but I, um. . ." Here he hesitated, albeit slightly. "I guess I should tell you that I have a few wrinkles to iron out first."

"Wrinkles?"

"I'm dealing with a probate issue related to the property."

"What?" Katie felt her stomach twist in knots. "Are you saying the house is still tied up in probate? That it's not techni-cally yours?"

"Well, I think I told you this was my mother's property before she passed. She left it to me. I'm an only child and the executor of her will."

"Yes"—she tried to maintain her cool—"but I had no idea it was still in probate. I would *never* have listed it. That's. . . unethical."

"You'll have to forgive me, Ms. Walken. I've never been in

this position before. I'm sure you heard the part where I said I lost my mother."

"Yes." She swallowed hard, memories of Datt surfacing. How would she feel if someone confronted her on something related to his death, after all? She tried to soften her approach. "I'm sorry. Really I am."

"I've never been down this road before," he explained. "I went ahead and contacted a Realtor because I'd been told it was just a matter of time before the property would be released to me. To be quite honest, I didn't think we'd receive an offer so soon. You're really good at what you do."

Katie opted to let his flattery slide right by her. She needed to stay focused on the issue at hand.

"I figured the whole thing would be settled before the first showing. Turns out, settling the estate is a bit more complicated than I thought, especially without a probate attorney. Guess I should've hired one."

Oh no. Please don't tell me this.

Brian Hamilton continued on, his voice never wavering. "A savvy lawyer could take care of this in no time, I'm sure. I hate to think it's come to that, but I might have to hire an attorney to get the whole thing squared away."

"Oh!" As she reached to look at her cell phone to get Karl's number, a wave of relief washed over her. "I happen to know an excellent real estate attorney, and I'm sure he's familiar with probate issues. He could probably get this settled quickly."

"Great!"

"In the meantime, we're going to have to stop the process. You know that, right?"

He dove into an argument, claiming that the whole thing would be dealt with by the time they went to closing, but Katie knew better. She would have to pull the listing, at least for now.

She didn't want to alarm her potential buyers. But surely they would wait a few weeks longer to officially make an offer if they really wanted the house badly enough.

Katie committed the whole thing to prayer. God had brought this amazing property to her, hadn't He? Surely He would see fit to help her with its sale, no matter what road bumps might get in the way.

❧

Karl approached the pastor's office a little unnerved. From what Jay had told him over the phone, the church was about to be embroiled in a serious legal mess. And, from the looks of things, Karl would likely end up smack dab in the middle of it. He didn't have to get involved, but with so much at risk for his church family, he needed to make himself available, even if it took him away from his other work.

After rapping on the door, he heard Jay's familiar voice call out, "Come on in, Karl. It's open."

He entered the small office, sensing the tension in the air. Looking beyond the stacks of books and papers on the cluttered desk, Karl took note of the concern etched into the forehead of his good friend.

"You look terrible," he offered.

"Thanks." Jay sighed. "I know what the Bible says about not worrying, but I'm having a hard time with this one." He shook his head and looked Karl in the eye. "I wouldn't tell that to just anyone, you know."

"I know. But who could blame you?" Karl opened his briefcase and pulled out his digital recorder. "Do you mind if I record our conversation? No one will ever hear this but me. I just like to go back over things when I get home, and that's tougher to do with handwritten notes because I don't always catch everything."

"Sure, I've got nothing to hide."

"I only know what you told me on the phone," Karl said as he fumbled with the recorder in an attempt to get it to come on. "When Mildred Hamilton passed away, she left the church a piece of property out on the lake."

"Yes."

Karl smiled as he remembered the elderly Mrs. Hamilton. She always had an impish grin on her face and a finger in every pie. The four-foot-eleven dynamo had headed up everything from the benevolence ministry to the prayer team over her many decades at Grace Fellowship. The only thing church leaders hadn't let her do was drive the church bus. And since her passing a few months ago, she had been sorely missed by all.

Jay let out a sigh. "I know how much this meant to her— making sure the church had the property for our new facility. We discussed it at length. It had always been her plan to leave it to the church. She figured the house could be used for a parsonage. In fact, it's large enough that it could be used for both a parsonage and a retreat center for missionaries on furlough. There are acres and acres of prime land that would be perfect for the new sanctuary, parking lot, gym. . . everything."

"And now someone in the family is trying to sell it out from underneath you?"

"Her son." Jay shook his head. "He's a nice enough guy. Lives in Texas. Doesn't have any plans to move onto the property himself, so it's not an emotional issue for him. From what I understand, he and his mother were distant. Not really estranged, but he rarely showed up to help her, even toward the end."

"So he just wants the funds from the sale."

"Looks that way." Jay shrugged. "Though it's not my place to say. I certainly don't know his heart. But it seems mighty strange that he's shown up now, after her death, and not before."

"You're sure the property isn't already in his name? Maybe she was just living there but didn't own it outright?"

"Oh, the house was definitely in Mildred's name." Jay sighed and raked his fingers through his hair. "And the donation of the property is clearly stated in her will. I have a copy. But her son claims to have a different will, one that names him as the beneficiary of the land."

"Have you seen his version?" Karl asked.

"I haven't." Jay drew in a deep breath. "And I suppose it's possible that Mildred drew up another one I knew nothing about, though she talked about that new facility right up until the day she passed away. So the whole thing just smells—"

Karl almost envisioned the smallmouth bass Katie had tossed back into the creek as he responded with, "Fishy?"

"Yes. And here's the thing. Let's say the will her son has in his possession *is* older than the one we have. Even then we're going to have problems, because this guy intimated that Mildred was coerced into making the donation to the church, and that she wasn't in her right mind when she made it."

Karl couldn't help but laugh at that. Mildred had been in her right mind, to be sure—and happy to give folks a piece of it, which she did regularly.

He pulled out a pen and paper, preparing to hear more. "Surely there were witnesses to the version of the will that the church has in its possession?"

"Yes, but all three were church members, and from what I've been told, that's not going to look very good. I wish we'd thought of it at the time." Jay went off on a tangent, expressing his many regrets over that particular decision.

Karl did his best to calm his friend. "Still, those individuals aren't direct beneficiaries, so it shouldn't be an issue."

"Well, that's good. I guess." Jay rubbed his brow with his palm, but the wrinkles only deepened.

After pausing to think things through, Karl prepared to get to work. "Okay. I need you to be more specific now. I need names. Facts. Dates. Details. And I'll need to see a copy of the will, if you have it handy. And Jay. . ."

"Yes?"

"Most estates take months to settle. Years even. We refer to this as a probate gap. I can guarantee your patience is going to be tried as this thing moves forward. Just be prepared for that."

Jay let out an exhausted sigh then spent the next half hour filling Karl in on every detail. When and where the will was signed. Who witnessed it. Mildred's final instructions upon her deathbed. The location of the property. The appraised value. The full name of Mildred's son, along with contact information.

And the name of the Realtor who'd listed the property about a week ago.

It wasn't until Karl heard Katie Walken's name that he realized just what a pickle he'd gotten himself into.

fourteen

Katie decided to take a stiff upper lip approach to the Hamilton property. She removed the listing at once, fighting the sick feeling that washed over her at the loss of such a hefty commission. *It's just for a few weeks*, she reminded herself. Afterward, she telephoned the Morrisons, bringing them up to date on the issues surrounding the property. They opted to wait it out, even if it took weeks. They wanted the house. Period.

Though this whole ordeal would surely try Katie's patience, she made a decision to see it through to the end, no matter what. Surely the reward would be great as long as everyone's tenacity held firm. And she would eventually earn the commission. No two ways about that.

Katie was thankful her evening meeting was canceled, giving her a few hours to spend as she pleased. On a whim, she decided to stop off at an appliance supercenter on her way home from work. She didn't believe in counting her chickens before they'd hatched, but she did believe in being prepared. If God saw fit to bless her financially, whether it was next week or next year, what would it hurt to go ahead and start putting a plan in motion for her kitchen? She wanted to be a good steward of her income and would take the next few months to shop carefully, finding the best possible deals on every appliance. That way, when the time came, she would know just what to buy and from which store.

With excitement leading the way, Katie eased her way into the massive appliance center, unsure of where to begin. She'd shopped for a great many things over the years, but rarely refrigerators, stoves, and dishwashers. Thankfully, her condo had come equipped with those, but they were in serious need of updating. No problem—out with the old, in with the new. Right?

As she looked at the goodies in front of her, Katie couldn't help but think of her mother. What would it be like to go back to life without electricity? Life without a dishwasher? Of course, Mamm used bottled gas to operate her stove and refrigerator, but she still washed every dish by hand. Katie shuddered as she thought about that. There would be no going back to some things.

Pausing in front of a stainless steel refrigerator, Katie found herself captivated by its impressive size and appearance. She opened the door on the right and let out a whistle as she saw the space inside. "Man." She could put a lot of food in there.

On the other hand, living alone meant she rarely kept a lot of food in the house, didn't it? Why did she need so much space?

She opened the door on the left and gazed inside at the more-than-adequate freezer space. With such a spacious layout, she could almost envision it filled with all sorts of yummy things—ice cream, veggies, french fries, different kinds of meats, and so on.

And why not? The more Katie thought about it, the more she realized—*If I had this much space, I could buy in bulk and save even more money.*

Her thoughts began to shift, and she imagined herself married to Karl, raising a family. How could looking at a refrigerator stir up such imaginings? Still, she could almost picture herself reaching into this freezer to pull out food for her family.

My family.

Just as she'd done that day with the Morrisons, Katie thought about what it would be like to be married with a houseful of kids. All of the things she'd run away from years ago now held a delicious appeal.

And, ironically, so did this refrigerator.

Had the Lord really used a kitchen appliance to soften her heart? She had to laugh at the idea. Katie stepped back to give the side-by-side unit another once-over.

Just then her cell phone rang, startling her. Katie scrambled around in her purse, trying to locate it. When she saw Karl's number, her heart began to beat double time. How did he know she'd been thinking about him? Was he somewhere in the store, spying on her perhaps? Looking at appliances of his own—ones that put him in mind of a wife and family?

"Hey, you," she said, finally catching it on the fifth ring.

"Hi. Do. . .um. . .do you have a few minutes to talk?"

Something in his voice sounded. . .off. Wrong. "I'm in an appliance store. Are you okay?"

"No. I. . .um. . .I'm wondering if you could meet me someplace for a cup of coffee so we can talk."

"Sure. I can do that."

"Meet me at the coffee shop near the library."

She sensed something was wrong and didn't want to give up that easily. "Do you know something I don't? Has something happened back home?"

"No, it's nothing like that. Please just meet me and we can talk things through."

"I'll be there in ten minutes." Katie shoved the phone back in her purse and headed for the door, nerves leading the way. She couldn't begin to imagine what had Karl so upset. Something from work maybe? Regardless, he needed to talk to her, and she wanted to be there for him. Even if it meant interrupting her shopping spree.

Ten minutes later she arrived at P. A. Perk and noticed his car out front. She could see through the driver's side window that he sat in the front seat, cell phone in hand. The call must be serious from the look on his face and the tightness in his jaw. His wrinkled brow did little to alleviate her concern. If anything, it deepened, particularly when he looked her way and frowned.

"Lord, help me," Katie whispered. "I don't have a clue what I've done, but I have the strangest feeling I'm about to be taken to the principal's office."

With a heavy heart, she took a step in his direction. If she could've found an open window, she might very well have jumped through it.

❧

Karl led the way into the coffee shop and took a seat.

Katie gave him a curious glance. "You don't want to order anything?"

"Not really." The smell of coffee permeated the air, and he breathed it in, hoping for a few more seconds of peace before he split the room open with his news. "You go ahead and get whatever you like." He reached for his wallet, but she gestured for him to put it away.

She flashed a dazzling smile, one that nearly caused him to lose sight of why he'd brought her here in the first place. "I'm a twenty-first-century girl. I don't mind paying for my own coffee."

After a playful wink, Katie made her way through the crowd up to the counter, where she ordered something with foam on top. Afterward, she joined him at the table, taking the seat across from him. "Now, tell me what's happened."

He drew in a deep breath and tried to decide how to begin. "Remember I told you about that situation at my church?"

"The legal problem?" She took a sip of her coffee then made a face. "Ooo. Hot."

"Yes." He paused, unsure of how to continue.

"Is there something I can help you with?" She put the cup down on the table and leaned forward to face him eye to eye. "Need some sort of help on my end? From a Realtor, I mean."

"That would be putting it mildly."

"Karl, what's happening?"

He started with great care, guarding every word. "A few months ago one of the older ladies in my church—a Mildred Hamilton—passed away. She was a spitfire in every sense of the word. We're talking about a really generous woman here, one who stayed involved in a variety of ministries till the very end."

"Right." Katie gave him a curious look.

"Several months before she died, she drew up a will, leaving her property to the church. It was a godsend, because the congregation had almost outgrown the current facility."

"That was very generous." Katie shrugged. "She sounds like a great lady."

"Mildred was the best, in every sense of the word." Karl tried to swallow the growing lump in his throat. Clearly Katie didn't see where he was headed with all of this. "But the church has run into a problem."

"What kind of a problem?" She took another sip of her coffee.

"Turns out her son, Brian, has a different copy of her will in his possession."

The color drained from Katie's face at once. She put the cup down on the table, nearly toppling it over. "Brian Hamilton?"

Karl nodded.

"*My* Brian Hamilton?"

Again he nodded. "I just found out today. The will we have is recent, very recent, in fact. But this Hamilton fellow says she wasn't in her right mind when she signed it. If you knew Mildred, you'd know he's grasping at straws. I've never known a woman of her age to be so levelheaded. She knew exactly what she was doing and involved a great many people to make sure she did it right."

"Oh, Karl." Katie leaned her forehead down into her hands and groaned. "This is awful. I pulled the listing immediately when I learned the property was still tied up in probate."

"You did?" Relief washed over Karl. Maybe this wouldn't turn out to be as complicated as he thought.

"Yes. I would never have listed it in the first place if Hamilton had been straight with me. And I can assure you, I had no idea this was, in any way, connected to a disputed will. Or a church, for that matter. Especially your church."

"It's connected, all right."

Katie shook her head, and he could see the anger in her eyes. "The worst part is Hamilton led me to believe this would all be settled quickly, that the house could be relisted soon. I have clients waiting to purchase that house the moment it becomes available."

"If I do my job, it won't ever become available."

"This is awful," Katie said with a groan. "Seventy-two thousand dollars worth of awful. My commission just shot straight out of the window." She looked up with a stunned expression on her face. "I can't believe I just said that."

It took him a minute for her comment about the window to register. He responded with a simple, "Ah."

"What am I supposed to do? Lose the sale permanently?" She raked her fingers through her hair. "Brian made it sound like it would just be a matter of time before this situation would be squared away. He told me a good attorney could poke holes in—" Here she put her hand over her mouth, her eyes growing wide. "Oh my goodness."

"What?"

"When he told me that he needed an attorney, I gave him your contact information."

Karl let out an exasperated groan. "Tell me you didn't."

"I did. But, again, we don't really know. . ."

"I know one thing." Karl exhaled loudly. "I know that someone is trying to take advantage of my church, someone who only made an appearance after his mother died, not before. And someone who didn't think enough of his Realtor to tell her straight up she was listing a property that wasn't yet available. That's what I know."

"Oh, Karl."

"And I know that I've committed to help my pastor see this thing through to the end, which means I'm most assuredly going to end up in court."

"Facing Brian Hamilton."

Karl shifted his gaze. "And any Realtor who might try to move forward with a sale before this issue is settled. You can't sell a house from an unsettled estate."

Katie's eyes filled with tears right away, and he wished he could take back his insinuation that she might do the wrong thing. Still, it was better that she understood the worst-case scenario. If she or anyone else from Bucks County Realty tried to force a sale, they could all very well end up in court—on opposite sides of the bench. Better to duke it out here, in a coffee shop, than in front of a county judge.

Hmm. From the look of pain in her eyes, he might stand a better chance in front of the judge.

fifteen

The following afternoon, Katie sat alone in her office with the door closed, trying to collect her thoughts. She'd spent the better part of the morning on the phone with Brian Hamilton in confrontational mode. He admitted flat-out that he'd deliberately avoided telling her about the disputed will in their prior conversation. He also admitted his version of the will was the older one, written nearly ten years before his mother's death.

Still, he planned to file a motion with the court to stop the church from acquiring the land, claiming they'd coerced his mother into signing the more recent will. He insisted it would just be a matter of time before the true ownership was established, but Katie knew better, based on her earlier conversation with Karl, who had committed to see this thing through to the end. The two opposing sides would be hung up in litigation for months, if not years.

Katie grieved not only the loss of income from the potential sale of the property but the damage this had done to both her reputation and her relationship with Karl.

She thought back to his words about fighting things out in the courtroom. Did he really think it would come to that? Surely he didn't believe she would try to move forward with the sale of the property now, did he? He could accuse her of a great many things—breaking his heart, for instance—but she would never deliberately do something as unethical as that.

A wave of nausea swept over her as she thought about

Brian Hamilton. Now that she knew the truth, his whole story smelled contrived. Their most recent conversation had made things abundantly clear: he hardly knew his own mother. In fact, he could barely remember the name of her church or her pastor when pressed. He couldn't remember the date of her death, or even her birthday, for that matter.

Katie contemplated this dilemma from every angle, drawing only one logical conclusion. She had to talk to Hannah, and quickly. Preferably before Madison's birthday party, which was scheduled to begin in two hours. Picking up the phone, she punched in her cousin's extension. Hannah agreed to meet with her in half an hour, after taking care of some important paperwork.

During that time, Katie rested her forehead in her hands and prayed. She wasn't sure which hurt more—the loss of income from the sale or the look in Karl's eyes last night. Surely he didn't think the worst of her, not after the days they'd just spent together in Paradise. Still, the pain in his eyes surely reflected some degree of distrust.

And why not? Hadn't she hurt him before? Maybe he had a right to think the worst of her now.

With a heavy heart, Katie prayed. As the words poured forth, she did her best to release both the anger and the betrayal she felt. She also asked the Lord to guide her future dealings with Karl and to open his eyes to the truth—that she had meant him no harm. After a bit more wrestling on the matter, Katie also released her hold on any monies related to the Hamilton property. Clearly the Lord never intended that commission to come her way in the first place. Letting go of it, at least from a psychological standpoint, was the only answer.

As she wrapped up her prayer time, a knock sounded at the

door. "Katie? You in there?"

She recognized her cousin's voice at once. "I'm here, Hannah. Come on in."

Her cousin entered with a concerned look on her face. "You wanted to talk to me?"

"Yes." Katie released a sigh, wishing the burden would ease. "It's about the Hamilton property."

"Yes!" Hannah's face lit up. "I heard you've got a potential buyer. Congratulations. A family from California, right?"

Katie shook her head. "It's not that simple, at least not anymore. I had a potential buyer. Now I've got a nightmare."

"What do you mean?" Hannah dropped into a chair and gave her an inquisitive look.

Katie dove in headfirst.

After hearing the opening lines of the story, her cousin's smile quickly faded. "Oh, Katie. This is awful."

After hearing the rest, Hannah added, "There's nothing you can do. You certainly can't move forward. He can't sell a property that doesn't rightfully belong to him."

"I've already removed the listing." Katie shook her head, defeated. "And who knows? Maybe it really will belong to him in a few months, after he pays some savvy probate attorney a hefty fee to tear apart the church's case. But even then I wouldn't relist his house. I just couldn't do that."

"Because of Karl?"

"No." Katie shook her head. "I mean, that's part of it, of course. And I'm heartbroken over what Hamilton is trying to do to the people at this poor church. But primarily, I could never represent someone who didn't fully disclose something of this magnitude, even if the judge happens to move in his favor."

"Good for you." Hannah gave her a concerned look. "But I

know this has to hurt, Katie. I can see it in your eyes."

"I can't tell you what it's doing to my confidence to lose a deal this big. I guess I really had my heart set on this one." Such an admission was tough but true.

" 'The Lord giveth and the Lord taketh away.' " Hannah quoted the familiar scripture, and Katie's heart jolted. Hadn't she said the same thing the day Sara's baby was born? Hadn't God reminded her that He alone would fill the empty spaces? No commission in the world could fill that spot.

"I think I had all my eggs in one basket," Katie said with a sigh. "I really can't do that again. I counted on that money too much. Maybe God is trying to teach me something here."

Hannah shrugged. "One of life's tougher lessons, to be sure. But you're a smart girl, Katie, and a savvy Realtor. This isn't the end of the world. It's a disappointment, sure, but at least you caught this before Hamilton accepted the Morrisons' offer."

"That's another thing." Katie let out a groan. "The Morrisons. They're such a great family, and they *love* that house. They were willing to wait as long as it took. But when I heard what Hamilton had done to the people at Karl's church, I called them back. Told them I wouldn't be relisting at all. They were devastated." She shook her head, remembering the disappointment in Debbie Morrison's voice.

"So, you'll sell them another house." Hannah smiled, as if it were just that simple.

"On the lake?" Properties there were limited, to say the least.——

"The Chandler place is still available."

Katie frowned, thinking she'd misunderstood. "I thought Karl made an offer on the Chandler place."

"He withdrew it today, as well as his offer on the Wilcox property."

"Oh no. Poor Aimee."

Hannah shrugged. "It didn't make sense to me at the time, but I guess I understand it all now. Likely he considered working with anyone in our office a conflict of interest." A hint of a smile graced her lips. "But hey. . .don't give up the ship, and never underestimate the power of a mighty God. He can take what the enemy meant for evil and turn it to good. And you never know, the Morrisons might just fall in love with the Chandler farm. It's near the lake, too, and on some of the prettiest acreage in Bucks County."

"And much less expensive than the Hamilton acreage," Katie agreed. She was reminded at once of Karl's reason for wanting to buy that property in the first place. He wanted to see the land preserved. If the California transplants considered the idea, then Mrs. Morrison could have her garden and Karl would get the one thing he wanted most— someone who cared about the land and the home.

"If they go for it, I'll let Aimee keep the whole commission."

Hannah laughed. "That's a generous offer, and one I'm sure she'll debate, but the purity of your heart is evident, Katie." She paused and offered a pensive look. "And that's another thing. . .your motives have always been crystal clear. Anyone who might think less of you because of this situation doesn't know you like I do."

Katie shrugged. She wondered if Karl would ever see her as anything other than a money-hungry Realtor, willing to break the rules to get what she wanted.

Hannah gave her a wink. "Stiff upper lip, girl." She glanced at the clock. "Yikes. I've got to get out of here. I have to wrap Madison's present and then get myself psychologically prepared for twelve screaming nine-year-olds at the pizzeria. Are you still coming?"

After a quick nod, Katie said, "Of course. I wouldn't miss it for the world." An email from Karl had alerted her to the fact that he wouldn't be there, but perhaps that was for the best. At least Hannah knew the whole story now and had handled the news with grace and style.

With relief flooding over her, Katie gathered up her belongings and headed for the door.

❧

The following morning Katie climbed into her car and pointed it in the direction of Paradise. She had to get out of town, to clear her head. Sara's words still echoed loudly: "Still running, Katie?"

I'm not too proud to admit I'm running, Lord, but this time I want to run straight into Your arms. I want Your will in this situation. Save me from myself.

As Katie made her way out of Doylestown, she thought about the issues she now faced at work. Perhaps Hannah's response had been right: *"The Lord giveth and the Lord taketh away."* God had given her so many amazing opportunities over the years. She'd been blessed time and time again, not just with the sale of homes, but in so many other ways. And yet she'd faced several losses, as well.

As she contemplated her losses of late, Katie's thoughts went to Brian Hamilton. She began to pray for him. That he would come to his senses and do the right thing. That the Lord would intervene and soften his heart toward the church. That Karl wouldn't have to face him in court.

And as she drove, Katie prayed for something else, too. For the first time ever, she prayed that Karl would figure out she had left town. . .and this time, come running after her.

❧

After an extensive night of wrestling with the sheets, Karl

awoke to a slit of sunlight peeking through his bedroom curtains. He squinted and closed his eyes. As he filtered through the dozens of thoughts in his head, only one rose to the surface. He had to call Katie, and he had to call her now. Somehow he must undo any damage he'd done with his earlier insinuations.

He tried her home phone, but she didn't answer. Afterward, he signed online to see if he could locate her there. Nothing. Finally, he punched in her cell number.

She answered on the third ring with a tentative, "Hello?"

"Katie?"

"Yes?"

He paused as he heard the strain of a familiar worship song playing in the background. "I'm glad I got you. I really want to talk to you." The sound of a horn honking in the background threw him for a second. "Are you in the car?"

"Yeah. I'm headed home."

"Home?" His heart began to work overtime. "Spending the weekend with your family?"

"I thought that would be a good idea."

Except that it foils my plan. "I'm sure your mamm will enjoy having you."

"She doesn't know I'm coming. I might make a couple of stops first, do a little shopping. And, to be honest, I'm not sure if I'm going to stay at her house. I'm just feeling a little. . . unsettled. I had to get away from Doylestown for a while."

"Because of me?"

"No. Just everything."

"Katie, I really need to talk to you. I feel awful about something I said. I made it sound as if I thought you might deliberately do the wrong thing, and I'm sorry about that. I know you better than that."

He heard the break in her voice as she responded. "You. . . you don't know me at all, Karl. I've never let you know me."

I want to. The words got stuck in his throat. Perhaps they couldn't find their way across the huge lump that suddenly rose up at the idea of not having a chance to win her heart. Just the thought of it broke his. He'd already lost her once.

He wasn't going to lose her again.

sixteen

As Katie neared the Amish country, she opted for a slight detour before heading to the farm. For whatever reason, she felt drawn to a group of shops several miles away from Paradise. A tourist trap, that's what Mamm had always called it. A place for the Englishers to stop and gawk. To take photographs and ponder the oddities of the Amish lifestyle.

Today, however, the whole thing just seemed quaint. The growth of the community astounded her. Shops presenting everything from fudge to dresses, candles to quilts had sprung up. Parking lots, filled with cars and tourist buses, stood next to acres and acres of beautiful green countryside. Ironic, the two coexisting alongside each another. Was such a thing really possible?

And how interesting, to suddenly see things from the opposite point of view. As a child, she'd been the object of stares and whispers from tourists. Today she found herself gazing with curiosity at the workers in the shops. Had it really been twelve long years since she'd been in their spot? Did they feel as awkward as she did now? If so, they certainly didn't let it show.

Katie shook off these questions and made her way through several of the stores, taking her time to really breathe in the ambiance. On and on she walked, taking her time, drinking it in. Her past. Their present. Merging the two felt more comfortable with each passing minute. And the minutes passed with ease here, unlike in the city. Here people strolled about, laughing, talking, and shopping.

She made it a point to do the same. Today was all about rest and reflection. And good food.

After stopping off for an apple fritter, which she quickly consumed, Katie entered the candy store, ready to do some serious shopping. This had always been one of her favorite places, though the fudge in this shop could hardly compare with Aunt Emma's.

At once, Katie thought of Hannah and the unmended fences between the two women. Mother and daughter had hardly spoken in years, and all because of rules and regulations. Katie prayed for a miracle in that situation and also prayed that her recent run-in with Karl wouldn't cause a rift of such immense proportions. It would take a great deal of time and prayer to heal something of that magnitude.

She redirected her focus to the candy. "I'll take a half pound of maple." She pointed through the glass case at a luscious brick of tan-colored fudge. "And a full pound of chocolate with pecans."

As she waited for the candy, her mouth watered. She would only pinch off a nibble from the maple fudge; the rest she would take home to her family. Emily would be thrilled, as would Mamm. The boys would probably consume most of it though. As always.

After finishing up in the candy store, Katie moved out to the hub of the shops, the area where an older fellow charged tourists for buggy rides. Datt would've frowned on such a venture, no doubt, but this fellow looked to be having a grand time. So did his guests.

As Katie walked, she noticed a clothing store, one she'd

somehow overlooked earlier on. She found herself staring through the window at the most beautiful blue dress she'd ever seen.

Wow. The soft chiffon overlay took her breath away, and the trim at the neckline only served to further draw her in.

For the first time in twelve years, she contemplated the unthinkable. *Blue?* Where she would wear it, she had no idea. Certainly it wouldn't do for work. But something about it called out to her.

I've got to have that dress.

To wear blue again would signify the end of an era. Was she ready to let go of the past and face a more colorful future? With a smile on her face, she pondered the idea.

Yes. Relief flooded over her as she realized the truth of it. *I'm ready.*

A familiar voice rang out from behind her, sending a shock wave through her. "I think that color would look amazing on you, Katie Walken. I always thought you looked especially pretty in blue."

With her heart now pounding in her ears, she turned to face Karl, who stood behind her with an impish grin on his face.

"W—what? What are you doing here? How did you know I would be—"

"I know you better than you think, despite what you said earlier. I know that you love maple fudge, for instance." He pointed to the bag in her hand, which she quickly tucked behind her back. "And I know that you could never resist an apple fritter."

"How did you know I ate an apple fritter?"

He reached to wipe a bit of powdered sugar from the edge

of her mouth, and she sighed, feeling like a kid caught with her hand in the cookie jar. Only, in this case, it felt good to be caught, even with sugar on her lips.

"I also know that whenever you got stressed as a teen, you always wanted to go to town, to the shops. Remember that time you snuck off and bought a pair of high-heeled shoes when your parents were at your aunt Emma's? You actually thought you could get away with wearing them."

Katie groaned. "I can't believe you remember that. I buried the box behind the barn with the shoes still in it. Wrapped the box in plastic, in case it rained. Those silly shoes are probably still there to this day." She paused and gazed at him in wonder. "But you haven't answered my question. What are you doing here?"

"You didn't think I'd let you get away twice, did you?"

The bag of fudge began to tremble in her hand, and she did her best to stay calm. Had he really just said that? Karl had come looking for her, just as she'd prayed.

"But how in the world did you find me in this crowd?" She gazed into his twinkling eyes.

"I move fast. Nearly as fast as you *used* to. Looks like I'm catching up with you." He gave her a wink, and Katie's heart flip-flopped.

"I'm glad you did." She offered up a shy smile.

"Me, too." Karl drew close, and for a moment she thought he would wrap her in his arms. Instead, a shopper brushed past them, forcing them apart. Karl shifted his gaze to the dress in the window. "So, are you going to try on that dress or not?"

She shook her head, suddenly reduced to a stammering child. "I—I don't need it."

"You might. Someday." He took her by the arm and ushered

her into the store. When they approached the clerk, an elderly woman with silver hair, she happily pointed Katie in the direction of the changing room.

With nerves leading the way, she slipped the beautifully designed dress over her head. Staring at herself in the mirror, Katie had to admit, she felt pretty. The color was just right, but something more jumped out at her. It had more to do with how she felt, not how she looked.

As the "I'm happy in blue" truth registered, something amazing happened in her heart. Joy took over, and before long, giggling followed.

"Everything okay in there?" She heard Karl's voice ring out.

"Mmm. . .yeah." She twirled around to see the dress from the back. Another giggle erupted. "I like it."

"Come on out and let me have a look."

She felt her cheeks warm. "Oh no, I'd feel silly." *Happy, but silly.*

"Katie. I'm not moving until you come out."

She laughed. Some things hadn't changed. He still had the patience of Job, with or without a fishing pole in his hands. Katie gave herself another quick glance, then pulled back the curtain and stepped out into the store, curious as to what he would say when he saw her.

Karl took one look at her and let out a whistle. "Katie." He shook his head and stared. "You look. . ."

"Ridiculous?"

"Um. . .no."

"Amish?"

He laughed. "Hardly. But I've got to say, you look like something straight out of paradise." He drew near, and Katie felt his breath warm on her cheek. "Katie Walken. . ."

"Yes?"

He gently traced the freckles on the end of her nose with his fingertip. "I can't tell you how long I've waited to do this."

Her heart fluttered, and she looked around the shop to make sure no one else was watching. "D–do what?"

He slipped an arm around her waist and drew her to himself, planting a row of kisses along her hairline. She felt her legs turn to mush and thought for a moment she must be dreaming this. Only a dream could feel this wonderful. She closed her eyes to ponder that possibility then opened them to double-check the reality.

Nope. Not a dream. Karl gazed at her with the most hypnotic look, one that left her speechless, a rarity.

"I like you in blue," he whispered in her ear.

"O–oh?"

He lifted her chin with his fingertips and forced her to stare into his eyes. Beautiful blue twinkling eyes. Eyes she'd avoided for twelve years. As he leaned in to kiss her—right there in front of anyone who might be looking—she gave herself over to the sheer joy of the moment. Their lips met for the sweetest kiss she ever could have imagined, one most assuredly worth waiting for.

After just a few seconds, she felt the presence of someone nearby and took a step back, her cheeks growing warm. The clerk flashed a wide smile and spoke with a sigh in her voice. "Ah, to be young again."

The words made Katie want to laugh. Being with Karl *did* make her feel young again. And wrapped up in his arms, his soft lips brushing against hers, she finally felt whole. Complete.

Karl gave her a wink then glanced down at the dress once

more. "So, what have we decided about the dress?"

The clerk joined him, adding her two cents' worth, and before long, they'd both convinced Katie she must purchase it.

"But I really don't have anyplace to wear it," she argued. "My church is really casual, and we rarely wear things like this to the office. If I had a party coming up, maybe, but. . ."

"Regardless, that dress was made for you." Karl whipped out his wallet. "And it's my treat."

"What?" She couldn't possibly let him make a purchase like this.

"I'm buying the dress, and you're not going to argue. Remember, I just saved a fortune by not buying the Chandler place."

Katie let out a groan.

"And you just *lost* a fortune *not* selling the house on the lake. So, I think you'd better let me take care of this one."

She offered up a salute and a playful, "Yes, sir!" Then, standing back, she took a moment to collect her thoughts and her emotions. With her heart in such a state, she could barely process what had just happened, let alone where she might end up wearing that beautiful blue dress.

On the other hand, what did it matter really? As long as Karl liked her in blue. . .she might very well wear it every day from now on.

ॐ

Karl couldn't seem to stop smiling. Not that he tried. But, as he paid for the dress, only the crowd of people kept him from screaming out, "She's mine!" He wanted to whoop and holler, to jump up and down, and to shout to the masses that the woman he loved clearly loved him back. That the Lord had truly redeemed the time they'd lost. And Karl wouldn't waste another minute lingering over anything in the past, including real estate disputes. God would take care of all of that anyway.

Karl simply paid for the dress and turned to Katie with a smile. "What else would you like to do today? You choose."

She grinned. "I've already done most everything. Eaten too many sweets, decided to give up on my moratorium against blue. Kissed you. I'd say it's been a pretty full day."

He drew near and pulled her into his arms once more. "Say that last part again."

"It's been a pretty full day?"

"No, the part before that."

"Ah." She smiled. "Kissed you."

He leaned down and pressed his lips against hers once more, this time not releasing his hold for some time. Karl found himself forgetting where he was. Not caring one bit who might be looking. He could go on holding the woman he loved forever, as far as he was concerned.

When he finally let go, he tipped his head back and gave her a playful wink.

"Whoa." She looked up into his eyes with a grin. "That's one for the record books."

"I just didn't want you to forget." He gave her a wink. "And now you can say I've kissed you twice."

"You've kissed me twice," she echoed, reaching for his hand.

And I'd like it to be a thousand times more, he wanted to shout. But didn't. There would be plenty of time for shouting later. Right now he wanted to relish every moment with their hands firmly locked together. He wanted to forget the outside world existed at all, that problems and real estate woes would ever again rear their ugly heads.

They browsed a few more shops then wove their way through the throng of tourists toward the parking lot. Karl nibbled on a piece of fudge, enjoying its flavor, then glanced up into Katie's eyes—eyes filled with love.

He found himself captivated. Hypnotized. And for a moment he wasn't sure which was sweeter, the maple-flavored candy. . .or the feel of Katie Walken's hand in his.

seventeen

Katie smiled all the way from the shopping center to her mother's house. Every now and again she glanced in the rearview mirror to make sure Karl still followed along behind her in his car. Just the tiniest glimpse of his face sent her heart soaring.

She thought back to the moment he'd taken her in his arms. The feelings that had washed over her far surpassed anything she'd ever experienced. Her heart, once hardened to the idea of love, had obviously softened. And oh, how wonderful that softness felt! How blissful! From the moment he touched the tip of her nose with his finger, she had melted like a scoop of ice cream left sitting in the sun. And that kiss—she'd wondered if such a thing were even possible. Now she knew it to be true.

As she drove, Katie prayed. She called out to God for His perfect will to be done in their relationship—to smooth over any troubled places, take care of any unsettled work-related issues. If the Lord could bring Karl after her, surely He could handle those pesky little issues. Never again would she allow her love for things to come before her love for people. Never. She would toss every commission right out the window before she would sacrifice her relationship with Karl. Or anyone else in her family, for that matter.

As she pondered work-related things, Katie happened to pass the same farm she'd noticed a week before, the one with the FOR SALE sign out front. Funny no one had purchased it, the land being so pretty and all. She thought of the Morrisons at once, of their desire to plant their family in a big house with sprawling acres. She could almost see herself in a similar frame of mind, running hand in hand with her children across the backyard of such a house. Someday.

Winding down the curvy road, she drank in the beauty of the land. How much prettier it looked now that Karl had kissed her. How much taller the trees had grown, and how much bluer the skies overhead appeared.

Bluer.

Katie giggled like a schoolgirl as she glanced in the rear-view mirror, this time looking at something other than the car behind her. The blue dress hung from a hook in the back seat, causing her heart to sing. Oh, the joy of it!

I own a blue dress. She could hardly believe it. And it had only taken twelve years to work up the courage.

She would wear blue every day if Karl would look at her with love pouring from his eyes. Blue shirts. Blue slacks. Blue dresses. Blue everything. If he would only kiss her every morning, noon, and evening as he had kissed her today.

Yes, she would surely wear blue.

She pulled her car into the driveway at the farm just as the late afternoon sun lit the fields with an amber light. At once Buddy rushed the car, his tail wagging. Funny to see the Amish dog so excited about a car in his driveway. He jumped up and down, offering his usual greeting. Just the sight of him made Katie want to visit the puppies once more, to see if Miracle had found a home.

As she parked, Katie glanced back to catch a glimpse of Karl pulling in behind her. She couldn't help but wonder what Mamm would think if she saw them together. Would she put two and two together and come up with four?

Karl met Katie at the door of her car, opening it for her.

She offered up a "Thank you" with warmed cheeks. How long had it been since a gentleman opened her car door for her? She couldn't remember the last time. In truth, the few men she'd dated over the years had been far more into themselves than she would've preferred, spending little time on time-honored traditions such as opening a woman's door.

Now, as she gazed into Karl's eyes, Katie thanked God that none of her prior relationships had worked out. She also thanked Him that somehow, in the grand scheme of things, Karl had managed to stay unattached.

'Til now.

Together they made their way to the front door of the house, where Mamm greeted them with a smile and a hug. "You're right on time. Emily is in the kitchen fixing supper, and the men are due in from the fields anytime now. Come in, come in!" She ushered them into the house, where they were greeted with great joy.

"Where is the baby?" Katie asked, anxious to see the little darling.

"Sara's in the bedroom with her," Mamm explained. She lowered her voice to whisper, "Nursing her."

"Do you think she would mind if I snuck in for a peek at Rachel?"

"Surely not," Mamm said. "You go on in there, and I'll put Karl to work peeling potatoes."

Katie turned back to look at Karl, to get his take on the matter. He followed along on her mother's heels, a contented look on his face—as if peeling potatoes was something akin to slaying dragons. She knocked on the bedroom door, not wanting to disturb her sister, but hoping for a moment with the family's new addition.

"Come in," Sara's voice rang out.

As Katie entered the room, her sister's face lit in a smile. "I thought I heard your voice out there."

"You did." Katie drew near and reached out to touch the wisps of Rachel's hair. "I had to sneak in here to see my baby girl."

After a few more seconds of oohing and aahing over the baby, Sara looked up at Katie with a suspicious gleam in her eye. "Was that Karl Borg's voice I heard out there?"

"It was." Katie tried to hide the smile but couldn't.

"Tell me everything." Sara gestured for her to sit on the bed.

They spent the next several minutes giggling like schoolgirls with childhood crushes. Katie told her sister everything that had happened at the store then confessed her feelings for Karl. All the while, Sara's face remained aglow with excitement.

"I knew it when you were here a few days ago," she said.

"You did? How? I didn't even know."

"Oh, Katie." Sara laughed. "You can't keep love hidden. You're like an open book, every time you look at him. And when he looks at you, well. . ."

"What?"

"Let's just say he has trouble finishing his sentences. Or walking straight. All he can see is you."

Katie contemplated her sister's words as she made her way back into the kitchen to join the others. She kept a watchful eye on Karl all through supper, noting the many times he glanced her way with a glimmer in his eye. She longed for a few moments of privacy with him but knew better. They would have plenty of time for that tomorrow if he stayed in Paradise through the night.

After the meal, Mamm shooed them off to the living room. A summer storm lit the skies, and Katie looked out the front window, a bit anxious. "Mamm, is there anything I can help you with?" she called out.

"I'm nearly done in here. You just make yourselves at home."

Minutes later, her mother joined them in the living room. As she settled into the rocker, she looked at Katie with tears in her eyes. "I'm so glad you're here, Katydid. I do hope you can stay awhile."

"I'd planned to stay at a bed and breakfast in town," Katie explained, giving the sky another glance, "but it looks as if I'll have to stay here instead."

"Well, of course you'll stay here," her mother admonished. "Why, I would never have you waste your money on a room in town when there's a perfectly good one here." She dove into a lengthy discourse about finances and one's ability to be thrifty, and Katie smiled. Some things never changed.

"Your datt would never let me hear the end of it if I let you spend money on a bed in town. Can you imagine the look on his face at such a suggestion?"

Everyone in the room broke into a lovely discussion about Datt, one that ended with tears in every eye. Katie tried to picture the look on her father's face at the news she'd finally kissed Karl Borg after all these years. Surely he would be grinning ear to ear.

After a few minutes of chatter about the new baby, Katie glanced across the room at Karl, who observed them both with a crooked smile. Oh, how she wished she could read his thoughts right now. After their kiss earlier this afternoon, he'd never left her side. With hands tightly clasped, they'd made their way through several more stores, finally landing in the baby store, where she'd oohed and aahed over a precious little pink dress, one she wanted to buy for Rachel.

Common sense had won out, of course. Katie knew that some things would never change—like her family's desire for the plain life. However, she also knew that several things had changed already. Her heart, for instance.

Yes, her heart had surely undergone a transformation over the past couple of weeks. In spite of her childish struggles, she'd finally come to grips with the fact: *I love Karl Borg. And I'm going to make up the lost time.*

And now, as she stared at the man she loved from across the room, her heart felt as if it could burst into song. She wanted to run through the field behind the house, this time with his hand in hers—not in mourning, but to celebrate the wonder of what she now knew to be true. *God has given us a second chance. And I'm not going to blow it.*

Her mother drew near and looked out of the window into the darkened skies above. Turning to Karl, Mamm said, "Looks like you're not going anywhere tonight either, Karl. We'll find a room for you, as well."

"Oh, no," he argued. "I couldn't put you out like that. Besides. . ."

Katie knew his thoughts before he spoke them. It would be inappropriate for him to stay in the house now that they'd expressed their feelings for one another. Not that anyone knew, but still. . .

"I can stay in the barn," Karl said. "If that would be okay."

Katie looked at him, stunned. "The barn?"

"Sure, why not?" He laughed. "Do you know how many times my older brothers and I slept in our barn as children? We never minded. In fact, the hay was softer than our mattresses. It won't be a problem, I promise."

Katie had to wonder at his willingness to do such a thing

but didn't argue. If he wanted to sleep in the barn, so be it.

In the meantime, she would enjoy their last few minutes together before everyone turned in for the night.

With a happy heart, she glanced across the room at the people she loved. *I could be very happy right here. Forever.* She looked over at Karl and added one final thought on the matter. *Right here. . .with him.*

＆

Karl sprinted across the yard with an umbrella in one hand and a lantern in the other. Under his arm he'd managed to hang on to a folded blanket. Avoiding the pouring rain proved to be a problem, but not nearly as tricky as guessing the location of each mud puddle.

Had he really offered to sleep in the barn? Karl chuckled as he thought about it. After years of city life, curling up on a bed of hay would be interesting, to say the least.

As he opened the door to the barn, he heard a low growl in the distance. He'd already been warned that a particular mama dog and her pups would likely welcome him in their own special way. "Be a good girl, Honey," he said in his most soothing voice. "I'm not here to hurt you. I'm just here to. . ." He glanced around, looking for a place to sleep. Finally his gaze shifted upward, to the loft. With a groan he approached the ladder and added, "I'm just here to catch a few winks."

With the blanket still tucked under his arm, he began the climb. Thankfully, up this high the dogs wouldn't be a problem. He prayed nothing else would either. Like bats, for instance. They had a tendency to make an appearance at this altitude, especially in the summertime.

Locating a spot off in the corner that looked doable, Karl eased his way over on his knees. No point in trying to stand;

the loft area didn't appear to be more than four or five feet high, at best.

After a bit of wrestling with the blanket and the straw, he finally settled in. From down below he could hear the sound of the pups nursing, and from up above, the patter of raindrops on the roof. He closed his eyes and leaned back, taking it all in. Something about being here, so close to the land he'd always loved, did something to him. Instead of resenting the fact that he had to sleep away from the house, he celebrated it. Surely God had ordained this.

And, as he lay there, cozy in the softly piled straw, a plan began to take shape in Karl's imagination, one that surely had to have come from above. He glanced up at the ceiling and allowed his thoughts to wander back to what had happened in the dress shop. Had he really kissed Katie—right there in front of an audience even? And had she lingered in his arms, looking up at him with love?

Certainly he had not imagined it. No imagination could produce such wonderful memories. She had really been his—if only for a few minutes. If only he could turn those few minutes into a lifetime, then everything would be perfect.

Karl closed his eyes and offered up a prayer of thanks to God for orchestrating the events of the day, right down to his night in the barn. Surely it was meant to be a sanctuary, of sorts.

Unfortunately, as his eyelids grew heavy, other, more troubling, thoughts surfaced. He reflected on the church's situation and the role Katie had played. Her sacrifice had been huge.

Of course, the sacrifice on his end might turn out to be huge, as well. After all, the church could hardly afford to pay him for his representation. Working gratis didn't bother him; Karl knew the Lord would provide for his needs. But making sure he gave this case his all did. With such a heavy caseload already, he would have to keep everything in balance.

Which brought him once again to the question of why he happened to be sleeping in a barn in Paradise when an ordinary night like this would find him propped up in his own bed, plugging away on his laptop.

From outside, the sound of the rain against the rooftop lulled, wooing him to sleep. Turning over on his side, Karl decided to concern himself with work matters another day. Right now, he simply needed to sleep.

&

Katie crawled into her bed—the same bed she'd slept in as a child—and gazed out of the window into the dark, troublesome sky. A flash of lightning streaked across the darkness, and she shivered, thinking of Karl in the barn. Of course, his willingness to sleep there had certainly shown his kindness and concern toward her family.

Funny. It seemed she'd learned a lot about Karl today. She rolled over and shaped the pillow to her liking, smiling as she thought back to the moment when he'd kissed her. Oh how perfect, how truly wonderful she'd felt in his arms. How right.

Katie looked again at the window, giggling. Had she really slipped through that same narrow corridor twelve years ago to escape Karl? No, she had to admit. She'd been running from far more than that. And how ironic that the Lord had led her back to the very spot where everything started.

Or maybe it wasn't so ironic after all.

eighteen

Karl awoke even before the sun rose. His back ached from the position he'd kept through the night, but that's not what prompted him to rise extra early. No, he had something else on his mind, something altogether different.

He rose from the bed of hay and made his way across the barn, bumping into all sorts of things along the way. If he could just make it to the door, perhaps there would be enough early morning sun to give him a clear shot of the car.

At some point in the night he'd come up with a plan that just might work, one that would set the wheels in motion for an exciting future. Oh, it involved a compromise, of sorts. And there were a few details to iron out, to be sure. Hopefully it wouldn't take long to get things squared away.

He reached the door and eased it open, then took a peek outside. As he'd hoped, no one had yet risen. Unfortunately, that also included the sun. With the skies above lingering between black and blue, he tiptoed his way across the yard, aiming for what he prayed was the driveway.

As he made his way along, the fresh scent of the dew on the grass threw him back in time to the many mornings he'd risen at this hour to tend to the animals with his datt at his side. How he missed those days, and how he ached for his father, especially now.

This morning, a variety of early morning sounds greeted him. Off in the distance a rooster crowed, and Karl instinctively whispered, "Not now!" He didn't want anything to wake the others. If they rose too soon, he'd be caught in the act.

He squinted, and his car came into view. Thankfully, he'd parked behind Katie. That made his getaway a bit easier. Still, he would have to pray for God's favor once he turned the key in the ignition. Likely the sound of the car starting would awaken everyone in the house, including her.

Without thinking about the noise it would make, Karl pressed the door unlock button on his remote. The beeping nearly sent him out of his skin. He looked around to see if the sound had caused anyone in the house to stir. No, thankfully everything remained peaceful and still.

He slowly opened the car door and slipped inside. So far, so good. He turned the key in the ignition, thankful the engine didn't roar to a loud start. Instead, it seemed to purr. Another God-thing.

Just as he began the process of backing out of the long driveway, however, something unexpected happened. Buddy, the golden retriever, appeared, barking like a maniac. Karl tried to calm him down, but from inside the car there was really little he could do. Instead, he kept easing his way backward, down the driveway.

As he neared the road, Karl noticed a light come on in one of the downstairs bedroom windows. Then another upstairs. By the time he shifted into drive and hightailed it down the road, nearly every light in the house had popped on.

So much for making a clean getaway.

ੴ

Katie watched through the downstairs window with a heavy heart. Karl must have wanted to slip away unannounced; otherwise, why would he have gone to so much trouble to leave before dawn?

The heaviness in her heart matched the weight of her

eyelids. She'd hardly slept a wink, thinking of the possibilities, of the life she and Karl could one day share together. The children they would have. The merging of their two businesses.

And now this.

I had it coming. I did this to him—got his hopes up then dashed them. Maybe it's payback time.

She thought back to their kiss in the dress shop. Was it all just an act, part of his plan to crush her hopes as she'd done to his all those years ago? How convincing it had been. The twinkle in his eye had drawn her in, like a spider spinning a web. And she'd apparently stepped right into it.

A rap on the bedroom door caught her attention. She quickly dabbed away tears and called out, "Come in."

"Katydid?"

"Yes, Mamm?"

Her mother drew near and lit the lantern on the bedside table. Katie could read the concern in her eyes. Mamm wrapped her in her arms and whispered, "I'm sure it's not what you're thinking."

After a reflective sigh, Katie asked, "How do you know what I'm thinking?"

"Oh, honey." Her mother laughed. "I know you so well. We're more alike than you know."

"We are?"

"Oh yes." A hint of a smile graced her mother's lips. "We're from the same stock, after all. We are both hard workers."

"True."

"Both extremely passionate and driven."

Katie gave Mamm an inquisitive look. She'd never really thought of her mother as being passionate before. However, as the thought took root, she couldn't deny it. Her mother's passions were for family, faith, and community.

"I guess we are alike," Katie said after a moment. Not that

she minded. There were few people she'd rather be more like than her mother.

Mamm smiled. "There are so many things I could tell you. A few might even stun you."

Katie turned to her mother, more curious than ever. "What do you mean?"

Mamm took Katie's hands in her own. "Did you know that I left the Amish country when I was seventeen?"

"W–what?"

"Yes." Mamm sighed. "I was in love. At least I thought I was."

"With Datt?"

A moment of silence was long enough to convince her otherwise.

"With an English boy I'd met in school," her mother admitted with flushed cheeks. "Back then, the Amish children were integrated into the public schools and learned alongside the English children. At some point in my midteens, I met this boy, Chuck, and fell head over heels."

Katie could scarcely believe this story. Her mother. . .in love with a boy named Chuck? Why had she never heard this story before? "He wanted to take you away from the Amish lifestyle?"

"That's just it." Her mother sighed. "He didn't want to take me away at all, but I was too naive to see it. I went to the trouble to run away from home, thinking he was interested in marrying me, and he didn't even want me at all. Turns out the other boys in the school had put him up to it—making me think he liked me when he really didn't."

"Oh, Mamm, that's awful."

"It was humiliating. But here's the funny part"—her mother's eyes took on a faraway look—"I left late at night, planning to meet him in town. When I got there, he didn't show up, so I located a public phone and called him."

"What happened?"

"Nothing. He told me the whole thing was a joke. Apparently the boys had placed their bait, and I took it. Anyway, I walked back home again, crying all the way." Mamm sighed. "My parents never even knew I left, and I never told them."

"You're kidding."

"No, but the Lord knew, and He certainly had a lot to deal with in my heart. The pain and rejection, of course. And then there was the issue of my leaving to marry an English boy. I carried quite a bit of guilt over that."

"Ah." Katie understood such guilt.

"The next morning I woke up with huge bags under my eyes and I was congested from all the crying. My mamm took one look at me and assumed I had the flu, so she started doctoring me right away."

Katie hung on her mother's every word, mesmerized.

"My heart mended, and the funniest thing happened— your datt's family moved to Paradise that same fall from Indiana. When I met that man. . ." Her eyes filled with tears. She took Katie by the hand. "I knew from the moment I met your father that he was the man for me. And I have thanked God every day since that Chuck Brower broke my heart."

"Like I broke Karl's heart," Katie acknowledged.

"Oh no." Her mother shook her head. "Karl was hurt when you left, of course. Like a wounded puppy for the first few months. But his wounds healed over nicely. Until his parents passed away. I think that was the thing that damaged him most."

Katie looked out of the window with longing. "I was so foolish back then, Mamm. A silly young girl who didn't know what she wanted." Her eyes filled with tears. "But I know now." She turned to face her mother. "And I think it's too late."

Mamm grinned. "Oh, sweet girl, it's never too late when the Lord's in charge." She gave Katie's hand a squeeze. "You just commit this to prayer and see what the Almighty does. He has a way of turning pain into something quite beautiful." Her eyes filled with tears as she gave Katie a kiss on the cheek. "If I hadn't met your father, I wouldn't have you. Don't you see? You have Chuck Brower to thank for that."

Katie giggled. "I guess." Her eyes now filled with tears. "But I'm most grateful to you and Datt." After a lingering sigh, she added, "I miss him so much, Mamm. And I regret not coming home more."

"You're here now." Mamm stood and gave her a knowing look. "And that's all that matters."

As her mother made her way out of the room, Katie pondered her words. *You're here now. And that's all that matters.*

With a sigh, Katie realized the truth of it. She *did* feel at home in Paradise. But what in the world could she do about it now?

nineteen

Karl drove all the way to Lancaster, the nearest big town, stopping off at a local diner for breakfast. As he ate, he put together a to-do list. A lengthy one. He scribbled through a couple of things on the list, but the others could not be overlooked.

Buying a ring, for instance.

He would have to do that, and quickly.

Leaning forward, he looked at the paper, deep in thought. The Amish didn't exchange weddings rings, so offering one to Katie in the Walken house was out of the question. He'd have to find a spot. . .just the right spot. And then he'd have to think of something brilliant to say, something that would seal the deal.

At once, the plan came to him. He'd take care of it, and in the most remarkable of ways. Surely she would accept the ring and agree to be his wife.

Now for the second part of the plan—the compromise. The part where his world would merge with hers. The part where they would both learn to lean a bit, meeting in the middle. Surely he knew just how this would work.

After leaving the restaurant, Karl drove up and down the streets in search of a real estate office. Thankfully, he located one within minutes. He entered with a particular plan in mind and exited nearly an hour later, joy flooding his heart. At this point, motivation growing, Karl stopped in at a pricey jewelry store, locating the most exquisite ring he'd ever seen, one sure to make Katie's eyes pop.

Now to perform the deed.

Karl drove to the Walken farm, praying most of the way. Afterward, he thought about the love he now felt for Katie. Surely it was a love born of waiting, but time had only served to strengthen it, not the other way around. And besides, he could hardly compare today's feelings to how he'd felt about Katie all those years ago. Maybe it'd been puppy love back then, the kind that would have blossomed into something more real in time. With the right circumstances. Maybe they both needed to see where life would take them as individuals before they could come together as husband and wife.

Was that the real message here? Had God used their time apart to grow them as individuals so that they would make a stronger couple? Karl chewed on that awhile. He'd grown so much since his parents' deaths. Might not make much sense to those still living in the Amish community, but his faith had grown in leaps and bounds over the past few years away. And Katie had clearly blossomed into a mighty woman of God, too. One who was finally ready to be swept off her feet.

He hoped.

His heart soared as he thought about the ring burning a hole in his pocket. He could hardly wait to present it to his bride-to-be.

His heart swelled at the idea. She'd almost been his once before, but clearly God had a different plan. They were both just children back then, not ready for the changes ahead. Now, older and wiser, they could face the future together. Like-minded. In one accord.

He reached the farm and pulled his car into the driveway. Buddy greeted him, of course, but so did a host of Walken family members, appearing on the porch the moment his car pulled in.

"Uh oh." None of them looked terribly happy. Maybe he shouldn't have left without telling anyone. Did they think. . .

He drew in a sharp breath as reality hit. *They thought I was running away—like Katie did.* A delicious chuckle slipped out as he made his way from the car to the driveway. *Oh, if they only knew!*

As he meandered up the porch, Karl did his best to play it cool. "Hey, everyone."

"Karl." Katie's older brother, Amos, gave him a stern look. "Urgent business in town?"

"I couldn't have put it better myself." Karl looked through the crowd to find Katie, but she was noticeably absent. "Where. . .um. . .is—"

"You looking for Katie?" Mrs. Walken appeared in the doorway. "She's in the field out behind the house. Want me to go fetch her for you?"

"No." He did his best to hide the playful smile that attempted to rise up. "I think I'd like to fetch her myself."

The twinkle in Amos's eye let Karl know he understood. With a wink to all family members, Karl trudged around the side of the house, through the mud left from last night's rainstorm, until he finally arrived in the backyard. He looked out across the field, finally able to catch a glimpse of Katie as she ran.

"Man, she's fast." He started to take off after her but decided to give it a moment. If she went out, she surely had to come back in, right?

A couple of moments proved the point. Katie turned and began to walk toward the house. When she saw Karl, however, her walk turned into a sprint. The sprint turned into a full-fledged run. And before he knew it, she stood directly in front of him, her breaths coming hard and fast.

He hardly knew what to make of the expression in her eyes. Pain? Betrayal? Hope? Excitement? Funny how a woman could say so much without uttering a word.

"Nice morning?" he asked.

The smirk spoke volumes.

"Feel like going for a walk?"

"I just went for one." She turned back toward the house, and he reached to take her by the arm.

"Oh no, you don't," he said with a laugh. "I'm not going to let you get away that easily. You're coming with me, Katie Walken."

Her eyes grew large as she responded. "Oh, I am, am I?"

"You are." He took deliberate steps away from the house, and toward the creek. Once they arrived, he would set his plan in motion. Until then, he just had to figure out a way to keep her feet moving in unison with his.

❧

Katie's heart thumped a hundred miles an hour as Karl led her beyond the field and into the clearing. Mud covered her sneakers. Nothing she could do about that. But after the prayer time she'd just had, her heart was as clean.

The first several paces were filled with questions. Why had he picked today, of all days, to run away and then come back? And what in the world was he doing, walking her through mud puddles? "Do you mind if I ask where we're going?" she asked finally.

Karl simply shook his head.

"Won't you even give me a hint?" she tried.

He responded by shaking his head. Then, as Karl's hand reached down to grab hers, as he turned to give her a wink, all prior fears melted into one blissful thought. *This is the hint. He's not here to break my heart. He's got something up his sleeve.*

As they approached the creek, Katie held her breath. Fishing? Today? Surely they couldn't fish, what with everything along the edge of the creek being so muddy. And besides, they had no poles. No bait. Nothing. Yes, something was surely up.

"Follow me, Katydid," he whispered as he led her toward the bridge.

Hand in hand, they approached the center, the same spot they'd stood at hundreds of times as children. This time, however, one of them did not appear to be standing. Katie looked down in surprise as Karl dropped to one knee.

"W—what are you. . ."

He reached to take her hand. "Katie, a man doesn't often get the chance to propose to the same woman twice."

She groaned. "I didn't exactly let you propose the first time, remember?"

He cleared his throat. "Um. . .no, you didn't. And thanks for the reminder. But you're going to let me finish what I've started this time, right?"

Katie felt her cheeks turn warm, and her hands began to shake in anticipation. Unable to say anything above the lump in her throat, she stared down into Karl's love-filled blue eyes and simply nodded. As if she would stop him!

She watched in awe as he reached into his pocket, coming out with the prettiest diamond ring she'd ever seen. Her breath caught in her throat as she took it in. He'd chosen white gold, her favorite. And the marquis diamond was flawless, perfect.

But not nearly as perfect as the image of the godly man kneeling before her now. And certainly not as perfect as the grace of an almighty, all-loving God who had brought them back together in such a miraculous way. She blinked away the tears so as not to miss a thing.

"Katie, I love you even more now than I did twelve years ago, if that's possible," Karl said. "I know we have a lot of time to make up for, but I want to enjoy every minute with you. I'm asking you. . ." Here he lifted the ring, nearly letting it slip out of his hand into the creek below. He caught it before it hit the slatted bridge, but not before Katie let out a squeal.

"Whew! That was close." Her heart began to beat faster than ever, knowing he would soon slip the beautiful ring on her finger.

Karl started laughing. "I can't even propose without fouling it up." He looked up at her with pleading eyes. "I'm trying to ask you to be my wife, but I'm not doing a very good job of it."

"Oh, you're doing a great job," she said with an encouraging nod. "Don't let me stop you." *Please don't let me stop you.*

"Katie"—he reached for her hand, slipping the ring into place—"will you do me the very great honor of marrying me?"

"Will I!" Katie let out a whoop, startling a flock of birds in a nearby tree. They soared away with their wings flapping in unison. "Karl, nothing would make me happier."

He rose to his feet and swept her into his arms. As their lips met for a magical kiss to seal the deal, Katie felt as if her heart would not be able to contain the joy. What she had ever done to deserve this she had no idea.

twenty

So here's what I'm thinking." Karl took hold of his fiancée's hand as they walked back toward her mother's house. "I'm thinking we're both a little homesick for Paradise."

"Are you suggesting we come back here to live?" Katie asked. "Surely you don't mean—"

"I'm suggesting we move to the area," he said. "I wasn't suggesting anything more than that. Returning to the lifestyle would be—"

"Tough?"

"If not impossible." He sighed as he thought it through. "There are so many things I want to do for people, and I know God can use my skills as an attorney." Here he paused, trying to work up the courage to broach the subject near to his heart. "But I've decided it doesn't really matter where I practice. And for that matter, unless your heart is set on Doylestown, you could sell real estate here in Lancaster County."

Katie's eyes lit up as she gazed at him. "You're really talking about moving back."

"I am, but only if you're in total agreement." He reached into his back pocket and pulled out a piece of paper, unfolding it. "I stopped and picked this up at a real estate office in Lancaster. It's a piece of property for sale not too far from here."

"You've got to be kidding me." She gave him an incredulous look. "I've been by this farmhouse twice. Both times it caught my eye."

"Mine, too, but I didn't want to admit it, at least not to

anyone but myself." He paused for a moment then added, "You know how I feel about the land." Karl tried not to let his emotion take over as he spoke. "I'm always telling people I'm not a farmer, but in my heart I am. I'd like to try something on a small scale, something that would allow me to get my hands in the dirt and still run my own practice."

"So you're saying you want to be a dirty-handed lawyer?" The corners of Katie's mouth tipped up in a playful smile. "You think that will go over well in this neck of the woods?"

After they both stopped laughing, Karl shrugged. "Why not? Maybe we'll start a new trend. And you. . ." He took her by the hand. "You will thrive here in Lancaster County. There's land in abundance here. Plenty to sell."

Katie shrugged. "Maybe."

"Maybe?"

"Well, I don't know. Maybe I'll turn out to be one of those women who prefers to have a houseful of babies. A stay-at-home mom." She looked up at him with a fascinating look in her eye, one he'd never seen before.

"You?" He couldn't believe it. "The girl who jumped out of a window in search of a bigger life? You'd be willing to stay home and change diapers?"

"Well"—she shrugged—"I'm not sure at the moment, of course, but maybe someday. And besides, raising children *is* a bigger life."

"True."

She leaned against him and kissed him on the cheek. "If our kids are half as troublesome as I was, they're going to need a parent to stay with them full-time, don't you think?"

"No doubt about that. But we'll find a good church to raise them in, one we can both agree on."

"Of course."

"And speaking of parents being close to their children"—he paused before unveiling the rest of the story—"the primary reason I'm suggesting all of this is because your family is here." A lump grew up in his throat and he did his best to squelch it. "My parents are gone, and now your datt has gone on, too. But your mamm is still here, and she needs you right now."

Katie's eyes filled with tears, and she gazed up at him with joy. "Yes, she does."

"And with all of your brothers and sisters nearby, I just think we'll be more at home in this area."

"You don't think it will be strange, since they now consider us Englishers?"

Karl shrugged and gave the matter some thought. "There will be hurdles to jump, no doubt, but they will be easier to jump from Paradise than Doylestown, wouldn't you imagine?"

"Yes." She gave him another kiss on the cheek. "I think you're brilliant, Karl Borg."

"Far from it." He shook his head, recognizing his own weaknesses far more than his strengths. "I'm on a learning curve in so many areas. But I think I'll be a better student with you at my side." He looked down into Katie's eyes and realized. . . he'd be a better *everything* with her at his side.

৯৯

The joy in Katie's heart consumed her all the way back to the house. She could hardly wait to tell the others. How would they respond? Emily would surely jump for joy. And Sara would be thrilled. Mamm. . .

Katie drew in a breath as she thought about her mother. What would Mamm think, after all these years? Would she expect her daughter to ease back into the Amish lifestyle then have a traditional Amish wedding ceremony? Katie had something a little different in mind, but surely Karl was right.

Perhaps they could merge the two worlds, come to some sort of comfortable arrangement.

As she thought back over Karl's plan—to move back to Lancaster County—a thousand thoughts went through her mind. She'd have to call Hannah, of course. Would her cousin be disappointed to lose her at Bucks County Realty? Likely, but she'd be just as thrilled to attend her wedding with the children in tow.

Katie smiled as she thought about that. If Hannah really came to the wedding, she would finally get to see her own mother again. Katie whispered up a prayer that God would eventually allow them to reconcile, for Aunt Emma to see the beautiful woman Hannah had become. And to meet her grandchildren. What a joyous day that would be—for everyone involved.

"A penny for your thoughts."

Katie looked over at Karl as he spoke the words. "Oh, I'm thinking about how good God is. He's already mended my relationship with my family, and I'm hoping He'll do the same for Hannah and her mother."

"Time is a great healer." Karl gave her hand a squeeze.

"Yes, it surely is." She pondered his words. Time had healed more than her relationship with her parents and with God. It had mended her once-shattered relationship with the man she would now spend the rest of her life with. "The problem with time is. . .there's so little of it."

"When you live in the city," he offered.

She laughed. "I suppose you're right about that. It does feel like the clock speeds up when we're away from Paradise. But I have a feeling. . ." A smile crept across her lips.

"What?"

"Well, I have a feeling the clock's going to move at warp

speed during our engagement. We have so much planning to do. We'll have to settle on a date and figure out where the ceremony will take place. And, of course, I'll have to find the perfect dress. We'll have to decide how many guests to invite then select invitations. And we'll have to talk about who will perform the ceremony. Oh, and then we'll have to see about bridal showers. Surely Hannah and Aimee will want to host one for me, maybe a lingerie shower at that." She dove off into a lengthy list of things they would have to do together over the next few months, totally lost in the joy of it all.

"Whoa." He interrupted her with a laugh. "I can't believe you're already thinking about these things."

Katie stopped dead in her tracks and stared him down. "Are you kidding? A girl has to think about these things. Why, I've been thinking about my wedding ever since. . ." She paused and put a hand to her mouth.

"What?"

"Since I almost married you the first time." She giggled.

"Oh, really." He pulled her close. "So you actually gave thought to marrying me back then?"

"I always loved you, Karl," Katie confessed with a sigh. "And what I said that night at the restaurant still holds true. It wasn't *you* I was running from. It was the lifestyle. Maybe I wasn't ready for marriage yet, but I am now. And I'm the happiest girl on planet Earth. I don't know if I've mentioned that or not, but I am."

He leaned in to kiss her then ran his fingers along the tip of her nose. "Well, if planning our wedding makes you this happy, then let's go for it." He chuckled. "Now, give me details. Are you thinking about a big fancy church in town? And if so, which town? Doylestown or one of the local villages near Paradise?"

"That's the funny part. When I was younger, I thought I wanted a ceremony with all the trappings, something a young Amish woman would never get to have. Fancy dresses, lots of bridesmaids, beautiful decorations for the reception hall, caterers, a huge cake..."

"And now?"

"Now...?" She allowed herself to dream a bit. "Now I think simple and sweet would be nice."

"Simple and sweet." He gave her a wink. "Kind of like the groom."

She reached over and gave him a peck on the cheek. "You are sweet, Karl Borg. You're the sweetest man I've ever known." Thinking she would catch him while the catching was good, Katie asked one final question. "Um, Karl?"

"Yes?"

Katie dared to brave the question on her heart, one she could simply not avoid. "How do you feel about golden retrievers?"

"Golden retrievers?" He gave her an inquisitive look. "To be honest, I think the breed is highly overrated."

"Oh."

After a wink, he added, "Unless you happen to live on a farm."

Katie reached up for one more kiss and whispered, "Thank you."

As he took her hand in his own and they began to walk together across the field, she was reminded of that little hummingbird she'd seen on her mother's porch less than a week ago. Katie now envisioned it returning to its feeder, its iridescent wings holding it slightly aloft as the slender beak dipped down into the water below.

This time, instead of taking to flight, he settled in, taking advantage of the sweetness. A feeling of peace settled into Katie's heart as she realized she'd finally stopped running. Finally stopped flying away.

Soon. . .she would be Mrs. Karl Borg. She would live in a house on several acres in Paradise. And she would do it all, after having tasted of the things of the world. . .and leaving them far behind.

epilogue

The following spring, on a particularly breathtaking Saturday, Karl Borg approached the center of the bridge at Pequea Creek. This time there were no fishing poles involved. Thankfully, he'd already made the right catch, snagged the one elusive fish who'd slipped away thirteen years prior. This time she promised to stay put. Forever. Today Katie Walken would join him at the center of the bridge and link hands—and hearts—with him forever.

With joy flooding his heart, he took his place at the center of the bridge next to Jeff Ludlow, who looked at him with a warm and inviting smile. Of course, Jeff had a lot to smile about these days, what with Brian Hamilton finally relinquishing his hold on the church's property. Still, Karl had a feeling Jeff's current smile had more to do with the fact that he was about to perform a special wedding ceremony, one they had planned for months.

As Karl looked out over the small crowd of friends and family members stationed on the side of the creek, excitement took hold. Somewhere, hiding behind a tree perhaps, his bride-to-be awaited. From what he'd been told, she looked like a million bucks. He could hardly wait to see the dress she'd selected, one—he'd been told—that rivaled any in a fashion magazine.

Suddenly, off in the distance, he saw a shimmer of blue. His beautiful bride came into focus, and he almost laughed at the sight of her. Instead of a traditional wedding dress, she wore the beautiful blue dress he'd purchased for her last summer. *Oh, Katie. You've done it. You've made your statement loud and clear, for all to see. You're wearing blue.* She drew near, making her way beyond the throng of family and friends.

Off in the distance, he saw Hannah and her children standing next to Emma. The tear-filled eyes spoke what a thousand words could not. He would have allowed his gaze to linger on them awhile longer, but his beautiful bride required his attention right now.

As Katie made her way to the center of the bridge, he couldn't take his eyes off of her. How many years had he been in love with her? Fifteen? Twenty? And how long had he trusted God for this moment?

Suddenly, the years melted, dissolving into a blurry haze. As he gazed into her twinkling eyes, Karl realized that time meant nothing. The wait meant nothing. The pain of losing her the first time around was gone forever.

Another thought surfaced. Surely the Lord had wanted—even needed—to let the two of them go through the necessary changes before they were ready for one another, ready to face life together.

Oh, but as he gazed into that beautiful face, he was reminded of little Katie Walken, the girl he'd waited for at the creek all those years ago. Her impish grin. The freckles on her nose. The sight of her sprinting across the backyard.

As he looked at her now, took in her beauty in that amazing blue dress, drank from the love in her eyes, he had to admit—no matter how long it had taken, she'd certainly been worth the wait.

⌘

Katie clutched a fistful of wildflowers in her hands, willing them to stop trembling. Oh, how she wished Datt could be here, to walk with her, arm in arm. She brushed away a tear and made her way through the crowd of people—beyond her many family members. Past Hannah and Aunt Emma. Past Aimee Riley. Beyond the Morrisons, now faithful friends. Straight into the arms of her husband-to-be, who waited with Jeff Ludlow at the center of the bridge over Pequea Creek.

If only she could get her feet to cooperate, everything would be just fine. Katie seemed to trip with every other step as she made her way toward the bridge. The shoes presented a bit of a problem, no doubt. Wearing heels to a creek-side wedding might not have been the best choice. Still, she had her reasons.

On the other hand, her clumsiness might have something to do with the fact that her focus remained fixed on the handsome man in the center of the bridge, the one in the stunning black tuxedo. Or maybe it had even more to do with the fact that he'd waited on her. For thirteen years he'd waited.

She would keep him waiting no longer. Hence, the clumsiness.

Katie stifled a giggle as she looked into his eyes. He'd clearly figured out the logic behind the dress, and the joy registered in his expression. *I'm done with running*, her heart cried out with every step.

She met Karl at the middle of the bridge, noticing at once that his gaze shifted to her feet. Yep. The same high-heeled shoes she'd buried behind the barn, thirteen years prior. Thanks to the plastic wrap and a sturdy box, they'd held up through the many storms.

Just like her relationship with Karl.

She flashed another impish smile in his direction, one that

spoke a hundred I love yous without saying a word.

Then, just as the pastor began to lead them in their vows, Katie's thoughts shifted to that little hummingbird, swooping down upon its feeder, drinking in the sweetness of the sugary water below.

This time the elusive creature had come home. . .to stay.

A Letter To Our Readers

Dear Reader:

In order that we might better contribute to your reading enjoyment, we would appreciate your taking a few minutes to respond to the following questions. We welcome your comments and read each form and letter we receive. When completed, please return to the following:

Fiction Editor
Heartsong Presents
PO Box 719
Uhrichsville, Ohio 44683

1. Did you enjoy reading *Out of the Blue* by Janice A. Thompson?
   ❏ Very much! I would like to see more books by this author!
   ❏ Moderately. I would have enjoyed it more if

   _____

   _____

   _____

2. Are you a member of **Heartsong Presents**? ❏ Yes ❏ No
   If no, where did you purchase this book? _____

   _____

3. How would you rate, on a scale from 1 (poor) to 5 (superior), the cover design? _____

4. On a scale from 1 (poor) to 10 (superior), please rate the following elements.

   ____ Heroine   ____ Plot
   ____ Hero   ____ Inspirational theme
   ____ Setting   ____ Secondary characters

5. These characters were special because? _____

_____

_____

6. How has this book inspired your life? _____

_____

_____

7. What settings would you like to see covered in future
   Heartsong Presents books? _____

_____

_____

8. What are some inspirational themes you would like to see
   treated in future books? _____

_____

_____

9. Would you be interested in reading other **Heartsong
   Presents** titles? ❑ Yes ❑ No

10. Please check your age range:

    ❑ Under 18   ❑ 18-24

    ❑ 25-34   ❑ 35-45

    ❑ 46-55   ❑ Over 55

Name _____

Occupation _____

Address _____

City, State, Zip_____

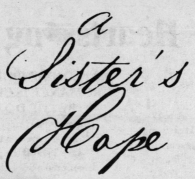

A Sister's Hope

Heartsong

Any 12
Heartsong
Presents titles
for only
$27.00*

CONTEMPORARY ROMANCE IS CHEAPER BY THE DOZEN!
Buy any assortment of twelve *Heartsong Presents* **titles and save 25% off the already discounted price of $2.97 each!**

*plus $3.00 shipping and handling per order
and sales tax where applicable.
If outside the U.S. please call
740-922-7280 for shipping charges.

HEARTSONG PRESENTS TITLES AVAILABLE NOW:

(If ordering from this page, please remember to include it with the order form.)

Presents

Great Inspirational Romance at a Great Price!

Heartsong Presents books are inspirational romances in contemporary and historical settings, designed to give you an enjoyable, spirit-lifting reading experience. You can choose wonderfully written titles from some of today's best authors like Wanda E. Brunstetter, Mary Connealy, Susan Page Davis, Cathy Marie Hake, Joyce Livingston, and many others.

When ordering quantities less than twelve, above titles are $2.97 each.
Not all titles may be available at time of order.